EASTON

EASTON

Glacier Hockey #1

S.R. GREY

Easton (Glacier Hockey #1)
Copyright © 2025 by S.R. Grey

ISBN-13 (e-book edition): 979-8-9926224-0-9
ISBN-13 (print edition): 979-8-9926224-1-6

Editing: Hot Tree Editing
Proofreading: Deaton Author Services
Beta Readers: Franci N. and JoAnna E.
Cover Design: Najla Qamber
Interior Design and Formatting by

www.emtippettsbookdesigns.com

Books by
S.R. GREY

Men of Fall series
Forward Progress
Fair Catch
Eligible Receiver
Down by Contact
Hard Count

Judge Me Not series
I Stand Before You
Never Doubt Me
Just Let Me Love You
The After of Us

Inevitability duology
Inevitable Detour
Inevitable Circumstances

Promises series
Tomorrow's Lies
Today's Promises

A Harbour Falls Mystery trilogy
Harbour Falls
Willow Point
Wickingham Way

Laid Bare novella series
Exposed: Laid Bare 1
Unveiled: Laid Bare 2
Spellbound: Laid Bare 3
Sacrifice: Laid Bare 4

Chapter

ONE

EASTON

Ten Years Earlier...

I glance over at my best friend, Claire, and for the first time since we embarked on this walk through our neighborhood to go down to the local park—something we do almost every evening when the sun is setting—she looks sad.

We were laughing just moments ago, but the vibe has definitely shifted.

I know why. It's due to the elephant in the room we've yet to discuss—her dad.

Last night, Barnes Weller made his annual pilgrimage from Los Angeles to Phoenix—in his private jet, of course—to take his only child out to dinner for her seventeenth birthday. Claire hasn't said anything about where they went or what they did, just that she's tired today since she got in really late last night.

Nudging her arm with my elbow, I ask, "Are you okay?"

Staring straight ahead to the park we just reached, she nods once. "Yeah, I'm good."

"You sure?"

"Yeah."

We start down a trail, and she looks over and smiles. But that smile doesn't reach her pretty hazel eyes.

Softly, I say, "Do you want to talk about it?"

She knows I'm well-aware her sudden change in mood has to do with her annoying dad.

Sighing, Claire kicks away a dried-up chunk of desert foliage that's in our path.

After a few seconds, she says, "There's not too much to discuss, Easton. Dad came in like his usual whirlwind self, picked me up in some stupid stretch limo, and then rushed us back to the airport. We flew up to Las Vegas in his jet, had dinner at a fancy restaurant, and then he brought me back. That's it. End of story."

I don't ask for details.

I know it hurts her that she only sees her father once a year, on her birthday. They text and talk on the phone here and there other times, but that's not the same, and it's not even all that often.

Barnes claims he's busy, busy, busy—his words to her, not

mine—running his multimillion-dollar aeronautics company.

He started that venture after he divorced Claire's mom.

And then it really took off, no pun intended.

The long and short of it is that business is his real baby, not his daughter.

I think Claire knows that in her heart, which totally sucks.

I've never met the dick, but I don't like him for that reason alone. I hate seeing my friend sad.

And sad is what he always seems to make her.

We're both quiet as we round a curve in the trail. Up ahead is a huge saguaro cactus with a funny bend in one of its arms that makes it resemble a person waving. A long time ago, we named him Stan.

There's a small picnic table next to the cactus that looks like it's been there forever and probably has. It was once dark wood, I'm sure. But it's been sun bleached to hell and back and is now gray.

Jerking my chin to the table, I ask Claire, "Do you want to take a break and sit next to Stan for a while?"

We sometimes do this, so it's not out of the ordinary.

"Sure," she replies.

We sit across from each other, under the watchful eye of Stan.

Claire's long hair has been up in a high ponytail held by some elastic band thingy—*hell, I don't know what they're called*—but she's now sliding it off and fluffing out her chestnut-brown locks, making the reddish highlights much more obvious in the sun.

I guess I'm staring, seeing as she catches me and stops mid-fluff.

"What?" she asks as she slips the band thingy over her hand and up to her wrist.

I shake my head. "Nothing."

Hell, I can't tell her I was just thinking about how beautiful she is, and how when she does that thing with her hair, my breath always catches in my throat.

See, we're just friends. We have been since she and her mom moved into our middle-class neighborhood five years ago when we were both twelve.

Secretly, I'm glad her dad didn't start his company until after the divorce. Otherwise, he'd probably be paying a hell of a lot more in alimony and child support. Claire and her mom would surely be living in some mansion somewhere.

Then I wouldn't know her.

Hell, I would've never even met her.

We wouldn't go to the same high school, where we share a lot of the same classes. Nor would we have started riding our bikes together two days after she moved in.

That's actually how we met.

We clicked right away. Maybe because we're both only children, I don't know.

Anyway, had we not met, we wouldn't be able to hang at each other's houses and do our homework together. Although, some days we slack on the schoolwork and watch stupid shows on TV instead.

I like those times best.

Anytime Claire's laughing and having fun, I feel so happy.

Isn't that dumb?

Oh well, whatever.

I guess what I'm trying to say is if Claire hadn't moved into my neighborhood, we wouldn't be the best friends that we are. Nor would we be taking late-summer walks like this one and sharing our lives.

Since I'm worried Claire may catch on to my sappy reminiscing—*and why am I doing this anyway?*—I clear my throat and say, "Man, I can't believe school starts next week. Summer went way too fast."

"I know," Claire agrees. "But this year should be fun. We're finally seniors."

"Right?"

She goes on. "It feels like the last three years kind of dragged. But I bet this one flies by."

Her pretty eyes meet mine, and I swear, even from across the table, I can see the cool flecks of gold and green in them.

Or maybe it's just me thinking they're visible, because I know they're there.

Okay, time for a subject change.

"And then it's off to college," I say, excitement building in my voice. "I know I tell you all the time, but, man, I can't wait to play hockey at Boston College."

It's true. I am fucking beyond pumped for this opportunity. I want to shine as a forward on their team. Hopefully, I'll make some good contributions and an NHL team will take notice of me.

Then the sky's the limit.

Claire knows my dream is to play on a professional hockey team.

Smiling, she says, "After you graduate from college, next up is the big leagues."

I blow out a breath. "Damn, I sure hope so."

"It'll happen," she assures me with another sweet smile.

I am so ready to go to college right now.

But there is one thing I'll miss—Claire.

With that in mind, I say, "You'll have to come visit me in Boston."

"I will," she replies. "Plus, I'm sure we'll hang out when you come home on breaks."

Claire is planning to stay here in Phoenix and attend Arizona State. I'm happy about that, because I'd hate to lose touch with her.

"For sure," I agree with a solid nod.

Sighing, she says softly, "Still, I'll miss you, Easton."

A pang of sadness hits my heart.

Running my fingers through my hair, I reply, "I know. I'm going to miss you too. Like, a fucking lot."

As the sun sizzles down into the horizon beyond us, painting the desert in shades of red, pink, and orange, Claire whispers, "You're my very best friend, Easton."

Her hands are on the table, and I place one of mine over hers.

Squeezing gently, I tell her, "You're mine too."

Flipping her hand over and entwining her fingers with mine, she says, "Can I ask you for something huge?"

We've never held hands like this, and I like it more than I should. It makes me want to touch her in other ways.

I quickly remind myself that we're just friends, and friends can hold hands without it having to mean anything more than mere affection.

"You can ask me anything," I reply, my voice kind of cracking. "You know that, Claire."

"Okay, here goes…" She blows out a breath, then says, "So, last night, my dad gave me the conditions in regard to when I can access my trust fund."

"Okayyy," I reply, confused as to where this could be heading.

I mean, I know her dad created a trust fund for her a while ago, but it's not like she talks about it very often. In fact, I think it only ever came up when she first told me about it, and that was ages ago.

Squeezing our intertwined hands, she blurts out in a rush, "Anyway, I get access to it when I turn twenty-seven. That's ten years from now. But there is one condition my dad put into place."

7

"What's the condition?" I ask, truly curious.

"I have to be married to get the money."

"Wait, what?" I laugh. "That's crazy. Like some fucking medieval shit or whatever."

"It is," she agrees, sighing. "But what can I do? Anyway, are you ready for my question part?"

I shrug. "Yeah, sure."

Her eyes meet mine and holding my gaze, she says, "If neither of us is married by that time, will you marry me, Easton?"

The amount of caring I feel for this girl is so strong that, with no hesitation whatsoever, I answer with what my heart is screaming for me to say: "Yes, I will."

Chapter

TWO

CLAIRE

Present Day...

After I take a small sip of iced tea and set the glass back down on the tile tabletop in the café where I'm having lunch with my friend Madison, I say, "Oh, I forgot to tell you. I closed on that big-ass house out in Cave Creek yesterday."

Madison's bright green eyes widen as she takes a big bite of her panini.

After holding up her finger for me to wait a sec, then wiping her mouth with a cloth napkin, she says, "Wow, no way. That'll be a nice commission."

"It sure will be," I agree as I spear an olive in my Greek salad. I then add softly, "God knows I sure can use the money."

"Right?" my friend says on a long sigh. "I hear you on that one."

Even though she was just devouring her sandwich, she pushes her plate of half-eaten panini away.

I understand why.

My appetite just went down the drain too.

We both sell real estate, and though we've had a number of good years, even winning multiple awards for highest sales, the market as of late has skidded to an almost stop.

Nobody is buying.

Well, they are, but not that much and not enough.

With my twenty-seventh birthday coming up, the only thing I can think about lately is how I sure could use that freaking trust fund money. I'm dangerously close to losing my small house north of Camelback Mountain.

And then there's my poor mom. She's been struggling for a while now too. She still lives in the same house we moved into when I was twelve, and though it's not huge, it's really too big for her now.

She'd be better off in a house the size of mine.

Hell, I could give her my freaking home if I had that stupid money.

Ugh!

The good I could do with that cash. And not just for myself

and my mother. I'd help out others, too, including Madison. She's been having a rough time lately as well. She rents a nice, roomy carriage house, but she's been talking about possibly having to downsize to a one-bedroom apartment in order to save money.

Damn it, see!

I need that freaking trust fund!

But I won't be able to access it this year. Not only am I not married, as per my dad's ridiculous stipulation and requirement, I don't even have a boyfriend.

There's nobody in the running either.

As of late, I've been out on a string of lousy one-off dates.

That's why I've pretty much given up at this point.

No man, no money, a faltering career.

Yeah, life is just peachy these days.

I wish my onetime best friend, Easton, had been serious about marrying me when I turn twenty-seven. That night, so long ago in the park on that warm desert evening, Lord knows *I* wasn't kidding around.

I had the biggest crush on that kid back then. Funny how he never knew how gorgeous I thought he was.

But I did think that.

Yeah, I was constantly swooning over his chiseled facial features, dark blond hair, cool blue eyes, and hot muscular build.

But that was really only the tip of the iceberg.

Easton was a freaking hockey stud. He was the best player on our high school team, and because of him, we went undefeated our senior year.

He scored so many freaking goals that the team went to some kind of state championship. They won that, too, thanks to Easton.

Amazing.

I was at every home game, and a lot of away ones, too, cheering him on. But there was so much more to my best friend than his good looks and hockey prowess. He was the sweetest guy. At least he was to me.

We lived in the same neighborhood back then and spent so much time together. I thought we'd be best friends forever, but when he went to Boston to go to college and I stayed here in Phoenix to attend Arizona State, we began to lose touch.

Then, before Christmas our freshman year, his parents moved to Boston to be closer to their son. He had no more reason to fly all the way across the country to spend time in Phoenix.

Space and time and distance came between us.

It didn't help when he found a girlfriend. I started dating some boy around the same time too. For me, that relationship grew serious, and the next thing I knew, our once daily calls and texts dwindled to the occasional "Hey, how are you?" message.

And then there was nothing, no more communication of any kind.

It's sad when that happens, but it so often does.

After college, I did hear that Easton had been drafted by the

Boston Bruins.

And then he was traded to a team in Atlanta.

The Thunder, I think.

I don't know much more, though.

And that's by choice.

It just hurts too much to follow hockey these days. It reminds me of Easton and what we lost.

It sucks, because I once loved the sport so freaking much.

We even have a professional team once again in Arizona. They're called the Phoenix Bears, and they play at the newly built Glacier Dome.

This season, which starts in a few more weeks, they'll be entering their second expansion year.

But that's about the extent of my knowledge of the Bears.

Again, by choice.

"Can you believe that?" Madison says, breaking me from my trip down memory lane.

"Wait, what?" I ask, utterly lost.

She narrows her green eyes and levels me with a suspicious look. "Were you even listening to a word I was saying?"

"A little," I hedge. And then I just flat-out admit, "Okay, no, you got me. I was zoning."

Madison rolls her eyes, but I can tell she's not really mad. She knows I'm always getting lost in my thoughts.

Slowly and patiently, she says, "Let's try this again, Claire."

"Okay, let's." Since the waiter took our plates away moments ago, I fold my hands in front of me on the table like a good, attentive friend. "I'm all ears."

"As I was saying," she begins as she tucks a strand of blonde hair behind her ear. "I have a very interesting showing coming up."

"Yeah, how so?" I ask.

"Well, the house my client wants to see is in Cave Creek, not far from the place you just sold. I forgot to mention it earlier, since I was too busy chowing down."

I laugh, then reiterate, "Okay, so what makes this showing so interesting?"

Raising a brow, she says, "Get this. The guy I'm meeting out at the property is a hockey player. Like a real live professional one. I'm talking NHL, baby."

"Huh," I say, nodding. "That is kind of neat."

"Right? Anyway," she continues, "here's the story. This guy was a free agent this past summer and got picked up by the Phoenix Bears. When I spoke to him, he said he's living in an extended-stay hotel at the moment that the team put him up in, but he's anxious to settle into a house before training camp starts. He really likes this particular Cave Creek property because there's a rent-to-own option." She shrugs. "I don't know. I just think it's kind of cool overall. I've never had a pro sports player as a client."

"Yeah, neither have I," I say distractedly, as I'm wondering who this guy is. I don't know, I just have a weird feeling, so I ask, "What team was he on before the Bears picked him up?"

Madison thinks it over for a beat, then says, "I think he said he was with the Thunder."

Holy crap.

My heart starts racing. "The Thunder, huh?"

"Yeah."

Sucking in a big breath of air, then releasing it slowly to calm my ass down, I ask as casually as I can, "What's this guy's name?"

"Easton," she replies. "Easton Sonden."

Holy fuck!

I need to play it cool. I'm not saying a word to Madison, since I don't know if I'm ready for her to blab to Easton that she knows me.

But there is one certainty in my mind—I sure as hell plan to find out if he moves into that house.

And then I need to know exactly where it's located.

Maybe, just maybe, if I work up the nerve, I might happen to be in the same area one day and show up on his doorstep.

Oh hell, who am I kidding?

Easton's had such an exciting life since we last spoke that he probably won't even remember me.

Chapter

THREE

EASTON

L iving in a hotel sucks. Even if the Bears did put me up in a pretty nice one.

Still, I want to get into a house.

That's why I'm glad I found a fucking sweet one up in an area called Cave Creek. It's a big adobe structure with an infinity pool and fantastic views of the surrounding mountains.

I think I'd like living there.

No, I know I would.

There are hiking trails all around the property, which is great. I can go on runs in the mornings and take a few evening walks, just like the ones Claire and I used to take.

Now *there's* a blast from the past.

She hasn't been on my mind in ages.

Though, to be honest, I've been thinking about her a lot lately. I guess it's because I'm back in Arizona, where we shared most of our teen years.

But nah, it's more than just that. Claire's twenty-seventh birthday is coming up on September 1.

That's only a week away.

Fuck, I'll never forget that date.

The plan was that I was supposed to marry Claire before she hit twenty-seven so she could access her trust fund.

Hell, back then, I would have said yes to marrying her for any reason. She meant that much to me.

If I'm being honest, she still holds a special place in my heart. She always will.

Too bad we haven't been in any kind of contact in years.

"How'd we lose touch anyway?" I ask myself as I continue to lie on the sofa, head propped up on a pillow.

The lights are off, and I'm looking out the floor-to-ceiling windows at the Phoenix nighttime skyline.

It's after 2:00 a.m., but I can't sleep.

That's why I came out here to the hotel living room.

I should try to get some rest, though. I have an early appointment tomorrow with a real estate agent named Madison to look at that Cave Creek house.

Fuck it, I'll just be tired.

Yeah, so why *did* Claire and I stop talking?

I guess, for me, I just got too busy playing college hockey back in Boston.

And she was here.

I think the boyfriend she had at the time played into it too.

And, man, that distance factor was huge.

Neither of us had any money back then to fly across the country to visit each other.

And when my parents moved to Boston before Christmas our freshman year, I never had a reason to come back.

So, yeah, life got in the way, and we drifted apart.

But damn, if there isn't a part of me right now that would love to reconnect.

Shit, though. She could be married.

For some reason, I hope the fuck she's not.

"What are you going to do?" I ask out loud, chuffing. "Marry her like you promised ten years ago?"

Yeah, right.

Then again…

Maybe it's the late hour, or the fact that I haven't slept yet, but for some crazy reason, I pick up my phone and look up Claire Weller.

Ahh, so she's a real estate agent.

And damn, from her business profile photo, she's still beyond beautiful.

In fact, she may even be prettier.

I should ask this Madison chick tomorrow if she knows Claire.

No, that'd be too weird.

I keep scrolling.

Hmm, it appears she lives in an area not far from Cave Creek.

That house I'm going to check out is looking better and better.

I can't find anything to indicate if Claire is married or not. Sure, she still uses her maiden name, but that doesn't mean anything.

The only way to know for sure is to ask her…in person…face-to-face.

Okay, I'm clearly just searching for a reason to go see her.

Maybe so, but who cares?

I'm not attached.

And hopefully she isn't either.

I type her address into Google Maps, zoom in on the location, and screenshot the results.

There, done.

Tapping my phone to my bare chest, I smile.

Now I feel like I can finally go to sleep.

Tossing my cell over to the coffee table, I roll onto my side and close my eyes, thinking about how, before September 1, I'm going to pay Claire Weller a visit and let her know I'm a man still willing to fulfill a long-ago promise.

Chapter

FOUR

CLAIRE

It's four days before my birthday, and I think I've finally built up the nerve to at least drive by Easton's new house.

Oh, he got it, by the way. In fact, he loved it so much that he skipped the whole "rent-to-own" option and just purchased the damn thing.

Must be nice to have those kinds of funds at the ready.

Anyway, Madison was all too eager to fill me in on the details of her showing with the "superhot" hockey player.

After she gushed about how gorgeous he is—which, to be honest, made me a little bit jealous—she informed me that he loved the place up in Cave Creek and signed the purchase agreement right there on the spot out by the infinity pool.

Since the house is already furnished, he moved in the next day.

That was yesterday.

After backing my car out of my garage, I stop in the driveway and glance up into the rearview mirror.

If I'm really going to do this, it's time for a pep talk.

"You got this," I tell my reflection, my hazel eyes peering back at me with doubt as to whether or not this is really a good idea. "Hey," I go on, forcing a smile. "It was in the news that he was picked up by the Bears, so if you just happen to drive by his house, it's not like you're really stalking him."

Though it is kind of a little stalkerish, my inner voice chimes in.

"Oh, stop. It's not like you're casing the place."

My eyes staring back at me tell me otherwise, so I stick out my tongue, then murmur, "Shut up."

It is so time to go.

Maybe the pep talk wasn't such a good idea, after all.

Ten minutes later, I'm driving around Cave Creek. I don't even need GPS; I know this area as well as I do my own neighborhood.

After a few turns, I'm on the street where Easton's house is, which thankfully happens to be barely inhabited.

As I drive slowly down the lane, I count only two other homes, and neither one is close to his property, which is at the end.

It's not really a cul-de-sac, per se, but there is a bit of a turnaround. I circle around and come to a stop across the street from Easton's house.

His place sits pretty far back from the road, which is good. It's not like he'll be able to see me out here, sort of stalking him at this point.

I breathe out a breath and kind of take it all in.

The house really is beautiful with its mustard-colored adobe exterior, dark wooden trim and beams, and clay tile roof.

The landscaping is pretty cool too. There are tons of small cacti and various other desert plants thoughtfully placed throughout his yard.

It's funny 'cause when Easton and I were kids, we always used to talk about how we'd love to have a house like this.

And now he does.

Good for him.

As I sit idling, I start smiling. I truly am happy that Easton succeeded in something he's always loved—hockey.

Okay, it's probably time to go.

I mean, I've seen his house, so I know where he lives.

But for some reason, this isn't enough.

I didn't think I'd be up for something as bold as this so soon, but I am—I'm ready to see Easton in person.

Part of me is curious if he looks the same. In the hockey photos I found online, he certainly still appeared to be hot.

But there was always more to him than that. There was a certain kind of charisma about him. He was warm and engaging, and you just felt comfortable around him.

I wonder if he's still like that.

"There's only one way to find out," I mutter.

God, I'm really talking to myself a lot lately. I know it's because I'm nervous. Speaking my thoughts out loud sometimes calms me down.

I think it's working today, but to be sure, I take a few sobering breaths.

Okay, good.

I'm ready.

After turning off my car, I get out, leaving my key fob and purse inside and keeping the car unlocked. It's not like this is a high crime area, and besides, I'm only going to stop by and say hi.

Then I'll be on my way.

If Easton questions how I know where he lives, I'll just tell him the truth—that Madison is my friend, and she told me.

After crossing the street, I step onto his property and then walk up the driveway that leads to the front of his house.

Man, there are a million things running through my mind.

Things like…

Do my faded jeans, strappy sandals, and frilly floral top look okay?

I think so.

I was going for a chic casual look today.

Wait, why am I even worrying about this stuff?

"Whatever."

Will Easton even recognize me?

Shit, what if he has a girl over?

He may not be married, but I'm sure he's no monk.

Fuck, this could be so embarrassing.

Too late, though, seeing as I'm now standing at his front door.

Still, part of me thinks maybe I should just turn around and leave.

This is so weird.

Or is it?

I mean, we were once best friends. He may be happy that I'm looking him up.

Gulping down a big breath, I hold it in as I ring the doorbell.

And then, exhaling, I wait.

And wait.

And wait…

Several minutes pass, and no one comes to the door.

Damn it.

Easton must not be home.

So much for all my worries and concerns, huh?

This was all for nothing.

Chapter

FIVE

EASTON

Today is the day—I'm on my way to see Claire.

Surprisingly, I'm not even nervous.

Well, okay, maybe I am a little uneasy.

But it's not too bad.

I'm actually feeling more excited to see her after all these years.

I wonder if she'll look the same. There was always something more about her, something not captured in mere photos.

I guess I'll know soon enough, as I'm almost at her house.

The GPS in my Range Rover directs me to turn left, then drive straight ahead about twenty yards.

Shit, I'm here.

Claire has a cute little place—a bungalow-style structure that sits back from the road. Not that she's on a busy street or anything. The area is basically a small suburban neighborhood.

It seems pretty quiet, too, as there's no one around.

Still, I better pull over and park.

I do exactly that, and then I cut the engine.

Now I'm a little nervous.

I look in the rearview mirror as I rake my fingers through my messy dark blond hair. Maybe I should have gotten a trim first. At least I shaved.

Yeah, all nice and smooth.

I also made sure to wear my nicest faded jeans and a dark blue T-shirt that my last girlfriend told me really brings out the color of my eyes.

Hey, she seemed to like it.

Maybe Claire will too.

Okay, enough stalling.

I hop out of my SUV and stride up to Claire's front door. With no hesitation, I ring the doorbell.

The nerves are dissipating. I'm now feeling pretty confident and beyond pumped to see my old friend.

But unfortunately, no one is coming to the door.

I try knocking, but still, there's nothing.

Fuck.

She must not be home.

My big plans are a bust.

I walk away and get back in my vehicle.

But I'm not deterred.

On the way back home, I think about when I should try this again—tomorrow, later today?

As I reach my house, I notice there's a dark gray Toyota sports car parked out front. It's one of those GR86 models. They look pretty fancy with the swooped hood and recessed headlights, but I don't think they cost a whole lot.

Still, it's nice.

But why is this mystery car parked across from my house?

There's nothing down here besides my home. Beyond the turnaround, there's just desert and mountainous terrain.

But, wait, there are some trails.

Maybe someone came here to hike.

I don't know.

Whatever.

Shaking my head, I pull into my driveway.

And suddenly...*fuck!*

Some chick with chestnut-brown hair almost steps into my path.

Good thing I hit the brakes and skid to a stop.

The girl steps back in the nick of time.

Damn, that was close.

With my heart racing, I place the Rover in Park and jump out to see if this chick is all right.

That gray car must be hers. Maybe she's a solicitor of some sort, or even someone from the real estate agency checking to see how I'm settling in.

And, fuck, I almost just ran her down.

Great.

This day is turning into a mess.

I rush around to the front of my vehicle, and the first thing my eyes are drawn to is how the girl's hand is placed over her heart.

I'm sure this is to calm herself down, seeing as I almost took her out.

Man, I do feel bad.

Just as I'm about to see if she's okay and apologize, I finally take a look at her face.

Holy shit!

Is it really her?

"Claire?" I say softly.

It is her.

This is not a dream.

Man, I can't believe it.

She looks the same, just a little older. But hard as it is to believe, she's even prettier, just like in her business profile photo.

Still, is this really happening?

Her hand is still over her heart, like it's frozen there now.

But then she looks at me and says, "Oh my God. Easton."

I think she's as surprised to see me as I am to see her.

But I don't know why. She is at my house, after all, which leads me to ask, "What are you doing here?"

Her face falls as she moves her hand from her chest and quickly crosses her arms in a protective stance.

I immediately feel awful.

"Man, I suck," I say, raking my fingers through my hair. "I didn't mean it like that. First, I almost run you over, then I make you feel bad for being at my house." I take a step closer, my voice lowering. "And, Claire, I don't ever want you to feel bad for being at my place. I'm fucking thrilled that you're here. In fact, I was just at *your* house looking for you."

Her brows shoot up, and she drops her arms to her sides. "You were?" she asks.

I smile. "Yep, I sure was."

Still seemingly amazed that I was at her house looking for her, she blurts out, "But why?"

Laughing, I shrug. "I don't know. Why not, right? I mean, I'm back in Phoenix now, and I guess I kind of was curious as to how you're doing." I raise a questioning brow. "Now it's your turn. Why are you doing the same thing? Looking me up, that is."

I really am amazed that she's here standing in front of me.

It's like a dream—a dream come true.

She shrugs like I just did.

Clearly, we're both nervous.

Softly, she replies, "I guess I have pretty much the same reason.

I heard you were picked up by the Bears—congratulations, by the way." I nod in response, and then she goes on. "Anyway, it's been so long. I just wanted to see you, Easton."

"I like your honesty," I say, because I do.

She nods. "This is how we always were. Honest with each other."

"True," I agree.

Her pretty hazel eyes hold mine, and she smiles.

Oh hell, my heart just skipped a fucking beat. She does still have that "something special" about her.

I smile back, and then, shaking my head, I say, "What a greeting, though, huh? You come to see me, and I almost run you over. I'm sorry about that again." I frown. "You are okay, right?"

I feel like a jerk that it's taken me this long to ask.

She waves her hand around and pshaws. "I'm fine, Easton."

"You sure?"

She laughs. "Yes, I'm sure."

"Good, good." I blow out a breath and then give her more honesty. "It is damn good to see you. No," I amend, shaking my head, "it's fucking great. Hell, you look fantastic, Claire."

She chuckles, and I feel like the ice is finally breaking.

"You look pretty good yourself, Easton," she replies.

I take a chance and walk toward her. She meets me in the middle, and we hug.

Fuck, if this isn't one of the best hugs I've ever experienced in my life. She's warm and soft in all the right places, and my body wants to hold her like this forever.

Okay, my body—well, certain parts—wants more than just that. But more importantly, in my heart, which is what I concentrate on, I feel all the caring I once had—and clearly still have—for my onetime best friend in the entire world.

And that demands more honesty.

So I say quietly into her hair that's warm from the sun, "I've missed you."

"I missed you too," she replies as she relaxes and melts into me.

Ahh, this is nice.

"It's been too long," I murmur.

"It has."

We stay like this for a while, just holding each other.

I don't know how much time passes, but we finally break away and take a very small step back.

Looking down at her, my hands still on the sides of her waist, I ask, "Do you want to come in so we can catch up?"

"Yes," she says. "I'd like nothing more than that."

Chapter

SIX

CLAIRE

He looks so good.

He looks so good.

He looks sooooo good.

It really isn't fair. I was hoping the pictures I'd seen of him online were touched up or something. And that maybe Madison was overexaggerating.

But no, everything is true. Easton is hotter than ever.

He's so tall and muscular, and his chiseled features are sharper than I remember. But his eyes are still the coolest blue. Right now they're really vivid, though it may be the dark blue tee he has on that's making them look so intense.

And damn, speaking of that tee…

Could his chest be any more sculpted?

Wow, just wow.

I'm in awe.

Easton Sonden is a man now, not a boy.

I like that.

Yes, I do.

But more than anything, I'm happy that it still feels like he's my friend.

I'd never do anything to jeopardize that. What we had—and clearly still have, based on the nice hug we just engaged in—is too special.

So when he asks me if I want to come into his house to catch up, I tell him, "Yes, I'd like nothing more than that."

It's the truth; I want to hear about everything he's been up to during the past few years.

Besides what I already know of his hockey career, of course.

As I follow him into his house, he asks if I'd like a little tour.

'Sure," I say.

I think this is his way to avoid any awkwardness. You know, keep us moving around to start off.

That's fine. As a real estate agent, I really want to look around.

The first thing I take note of is how stunning the interior is. I mean, the exterior is nice, but the inside is striking. I love the high ceilings, exposed dark wood beams, the spiral staircase in the back of the entry hall, and just how everything is decorated in a perfectly matched southwestern motif.

He only shows me the first floor, but that's okay.

We return to the entry hall and nodding approvingly, I remark, "This house is really nice, Easton. There's a great aesthetic in here, yet it feels nice and homey."

"I agree," he replies. "I liked everything right away. But I can't take credit for it. It came fully decorated and furnished."

"I know," I tell him. "I heard."

Cocking his head, he peers at me curiously. "You heard? How is that possible?"

I explain that I'm in real estate and Madison, his agent, is a very good friend of mine.

"Ahhhh," he says, nodding. "Now it all makes sense. How you found me, that is." Softly, he adds, "Can I make a confession too?"

"Sure," I say.

His eyes meet mine, and he shares, "I didn't know Madison is your friend, of course. But I did do a little research when I checked for your address. I saw online that you're a real estate agent. So, yeah, I already knew that part."

"Wow, that's cool," I say, smiling. "We were doing the same thing, looking each other up and stuff, and we didn't even know it. Well, I'll tell you one thing—it makes me feel like less of a dork."

That makes him laugh. "Seriously," he says, "same here."

Wow, not much has changed with us.

I'm thrilled he was researching me, just as I was looking for info on him. It makes me not feel like such a stalker.

We're still standing in the entry hall, and spacious though it is, Easton motions to his left and suggests we head into the living room so we can sit down and be more comfortable.

"Sounds good," I reply.

I follow him in, and we sit down on a dark brown, L-shaped leather sofa. I choose the shorter side, while he opts for the longer end. It feels like the perfect friendly distance.

Easton asks me if I'd like anything to drink, soda or water, but I tell him I'm good for now.

"Okay," he says as he props a throw pillow under his arm and leans on it. "I'm fine too. But let me know if you change your mind."

"I will," I assure him.

I feel so relaxed. This really is like old times.

And just like back then, we begin to talk about so many things: our college days, what we missed when we lost contact, some hockey tidbits that I didn't know, and finally, about life in general.

At one point, I think about his folks and how nice they always were.

That leads me to ask, "Do your parents still live in Boston?"

Easton shakes his head. "No. They moved down to Florida when I left the Bruins. I think they were tired of the winters, so it all worked out."

"Ah, got it." I nod, adding, "I'm sure they're happy to be back in a warm climate."

"Definitely," he confirms. "They're really settled in down there now. I don't see them ever moving again, especially not to anywhere that gets cold."

"Sounds like my mom," I share. "She'll never leave Arizona. She loves the heat too."

He's quiet for a few seconds, like he's debating whether to bring something up or not. I have a feeling it's about my father.

Sure enough, he clears his throat and asks quietly, "What about your dad? Is he still in LA?"

"He is," I confirm.

"Still has his company?"

I snort. "Oh yeah. And it's still his baby."

Another silent beat passes, and then Easton asks, "Does he still do his annual birthday pilgrimage?"

I blow out a breath. "He did for a while, but when I turned twenty-one, I told him it wasn't necessary for him to fly in and make such a big production anymore." I shrug. "He just does a birthday call nowadays."

Easton nods. "That makes sense."

"It does," I agree. "It's much less stressful."

He shoots me a sad look but stays quiet. I sense he's contemplating what he's going to say next.

Clearing his throat like before, he finally states, "You have a really big birthday coming up."

Oh, here we go...

"I do," I reply, keeping my voice calm and steady. "Four more days."

Like he doesn't know that.

"And you're not married," he continues softly.

I shake my head. "No, I definitely am not."

His eyes meet mine, and I swear that blue intensity is stronger than ever as he says, "But you could be."

Holy crap!

I swallow hard as I choke out, "What are you saying, Easton?"

"I think you know, Claire."

I blow out a breath, then tell him quietly, "I couldn't ask that of you."

"You're not asking," he counters. "I'm offering. After all, I made a promise, right?" His eyes hold mine, and I couldn't look away if I wanted to. "And, Claire," he goes on, "I always stick by my promises."

Oh my God, I think he's serious.

Damn, I want him to be serious.

The good I could do with that money—help my mom, Madison, other people.

Hell, I need help myself.

But I still can't ask this of him.

I reiterate that and add, "Easton, we were just kids back then when you made that promise."

"Doesn't matter," he says. "I meant it then, and I mean it now. So, what do you say, Claire Weller? Will you marry me?"

Chapter

SEVEN

EASTON

'm not kidding around or joking. I am dead serious when I ask Claire to marry me. I made a promise to my friend, and I intend to keep it.

That is, if she wants me to.

But seeing as her eyes are wide and her mouth is slightly agape—I think she's in shock—I clarify, "Um, you wouldn't have to do anything you don't want to do. Like, this would be a marriage of convenience, so to speak." I blow out a breath and continue, "I mean, I think we'd have to live together for it to look real, but you could have your own bedroom and bathroom and stuff. I'd certainly not expect anything from you, Claire. Like in a physical sense. We'd still be just friends."

She snaps out of her state of shock or whatever it was, but what's wild is I swear I detect a flash of disappointment in her eyes.

Is it disappointment that we'd remain just friends?

Nah, it can't be that.

I'm just imagining things.

In the midst of my overanalyzing, I hear the softest "Yes."

"Wait, what?" I blurt out, holding my breath.

I'm equal parts surprised she's agreeing so quickly and elated that she is.

I thought it would take more convincing. She must really need that money.

Or maybe, just maybe, marrying your best friend from the past isn't such a bad option.

But to be sure I heard her correctly, I ask, "You will? Marry me, that is."

Smiling, she nods. "Yes, I will marry you, Easton Sonden. As long as you're completely sure you want to do this."

"Oh, I do," I assure her. "I definitely do."

"Then let's do it."

Chuckling, I say, "Boy is your dad going to be shocked."

Grinning mischievously, she replies, "Telling him is going to be so much fun."

We share a laugh, and then we spend the next hour or so figuring out how we want to work this out.

In the end, we decide a quick Las Vegas wedding is the way to go.

Hell, I'm ready to fly up there tonight. But Claire suggests we wait until morning. She says she wants me to sleep on this decision to be sure this is really what I want to do.

"I'm not going to change my mind," I assure her.

But I ultimately agree to wait, simply because I want her to have the same option—to sleep on this decision.

After all, it is a big one.

But one I'm willing to make.

Damn, my seventeen-year-old self would be so excited.

But you know what?

My twenty-seven-year-old self is pretty pumped up right now too.

Claire doesn't change her mind.

And neither do I.

We fly up to Las Vegas in the morning, and after a quick stop at the Clark County Marriage Bureau to obtain a license, we check into a suite at the Bellagio.

I booked it last night, making sure that there are two bedrooms.

The plan is to stay one night and fly back to Phoenix in the morning. Right now this is all just between us. No one else knows what we're doing.

We agreed we want it this way. We can tell our parents, friends, and, of course, my new team after we're officially married.

And that's about to happen.

I'm standing at the altar in a cute little redwood chapel on the southern end of the Strip waiting for my soon-to-be bride to walk down the aisle.

The music begins, and shit, here she comes.

This is so real.

My heart is pounding.

But I'm smiling, too, as I watch Claire come toward me.

Damn, she looks beautiful in her simple but pretty long white sundress. Her chestnut-brown hair is down, which is the way I like it best, as it shows off the reddish undertones in her soft, bouncy curls.

When she reaches the altar, she stops and smiles.

The minister has us face each other, and we join hands.

We then recite our vows, which feels surreal.

It goes so fast, and as we slip the simple platinum bands we picked out earlier onto each other's fingers, I take her to be my wife, and she takes me to be her husband.

We're then pronounced as married.

Wow.

The minister says, "You may kiss your bride," and our lips meet in an uncertain but very chaste kiss.

It's done—Claire is now my wife.

Chapter

EIGHT

CLAIRE

"**N**o, Mom," I repeat for the fifth time, feeling more and more exasperated. "Easton and I have *not* been secretly dating for the past ten years. And no, I am not freaking pregnant!"

"Then why did you run off to Las Vegas to get married and not even tell me?" she whines. "Even if it wasn't the wedding I'd hoped for you, I would have liked to have at least been there to witness it."

"I know, I know," I say soothingly. And damn, I do feel kind of bad. "I'm sorry. It was just sort of a last-minute decision. Two old friends reuniting and realizing we have a spark. We figured, 'What the hell. Let's do something crazy and spontaneous for once in our lives.'"

"Well, it certainly is both of those things," my mom murmurs, still sounding miffed.

Not only is she upset, but skepticism is creeping into her tone.

She knows me and is aware I'm not Miss Spontaneous.

Though I guess now I'd be Mrs. Spontaneous.

Yikes, that sounds so weird.

Being a married woman is going to take some getting used to. Even if it is just a farce.

I sigh.

I'd like to tell my mom the truth, but Easton and I agreed we should pretend we have a real marriage for everybody. That way we won't get tripped up, and no one will give away our secret.

My mom is quiet, too quiet.

Damn it, I know she's catching on.

Sure enough, after clearing her throat, she says, "I know why you really did this, Claire. And I'd like to slap your father for requiring such a thing to access your trust fund."

I sigh again. "Mom, there's more to it than just that."

Okay, there's really not, but I'm trying to keep up appearances here.

"Uh-huh." She sniffs. "Sure there is."

She knows, but thankfully she drops the subject. Though I'm sure I'll hear about it again at some point in time.

But I'm safe for now.

To keep it that way, after we say a few more words, I wrap up.

"Thank God that's done," I lament as I toss my phone onto the coffee table.

I fall back on the sofa.

I'm alone and at my house. I came back here to pick up some clothes and things until I have a chance to move the rest of my crap up to Easton's place.

We returned to Phoenix earlier today.

The wedding yesterday was…interesting. I felt more emotions than I expected to, but I had no regrets marrying Easton.

I still don't.

He's just so amazing.

I can't believe he did this for me.

I was even sort of hoping he'd kiss me for real when we became husband and wife in the chapel. But it probably was for the best that he gave me a quick peck on the lips. I need to keep the situation in perspective. He did this to help me out as a friend.

And we are great friends. Still.

I can't believe how we picked right up where we left off so long ago. Within minutes of being reunited, it was like only ten days, not ten years, had passed.

So, yeah, I don't think doing what I had to do to access my trust fund is going to be all that bad. Being married to my good friend might even be fun. And being a hockey player's wife is certainly cool.

Speaking of my trust fund, the call to my mom was my second of the day.

The first one was to my dad.

Oh man, was he surprised to hear that I'm now married.

I think he suspected the truth as well, but he didn't outright verbalize it like my mom did. With a long, resigned sigh, he just agreed to release my money to me on my birthday, which is in two days.

I didn't ask about the exact amount I'll be receiving. I already know it's a lot. One thing, I'll have to hire financial advisers for sure.

But I want to keep an eye on what I invest in as well. That's why I'm thinking I'll probably leave my real estate career behind. I may go back to it at some point, but who knows?

Besides having a role in managing this money, I want to start and be involved with a charity of some sort.

It's important for me to give back.

I've already told Easton all of this, and he loves the idea of a charity or a foundation. He wants to be a part of it too.

That's great, as he can bring a lot of attention and visibility to any endeavor since he's a Bears player.

We've been discussing a bunch of ideas, and we're leaning toward creating a foundation to benefit the local children's hospital.

Nothing is set in stone yet, though.

So much is happening that we need to take things one day at

a time for now.

Nevertheless, I intend to make sure every day is better than the one before—for me, for Easton, for my mom, for Madison, for everyone.

Yeah, with what I did to access that money, life is about to get really, really good for a lot of people.

And that makes it all worthwhile.

Chapter

NINE

EASTON

Claire gets her money. And fuck, it is an enormous sum. I think even she was shocked. God knows I sure was.

I'm so proud of her, though, as it's only been two weeks and she's already doing so much good with it.

Since she lives with me now—with her own bedroom and private bath as agreed upon, of course—she was able to talk her mom into moving into her old house. She also bought her friend Madison's carriage house for her.

Poor Madison, though. She's still trying to process that Claire married me out of the blue. Everyone is kind of shocked. My parents too. But we're still sticking with the story that we reunited and sparks just flew.

In fact, I'll be reiterating that same thing today when I meet my teammate Lennox Foley for lunch. I'm ready because I'm sure it'll come up.

The Bears were really excited when my agent gave them the news that I got hitched. I guess they like it when players are settled down. Less chance for controversy, I'm sure.

In any case, they put out a press release last week that their newest acquisition tied the knot in an impromptu Vegas wedding.

So, yeah, now everyone knows.

I'm almost at the restaurant, and, man, I'm pumped to meet Lennox. Apart from being a new teammate, he's also the captain of the Bears. He centers the top line and asked if I was up for a lunch to get to know each other a little better before training camp begins, which is in a couple of days.

I like that.

I think it shows he's a class act, even if he does have a bit of a bad-boy image. I can see why, though. Lennox is a good-looking guy with jet-black hair and deep brown eyes. He has kind of a roguish look about him that the ladies seem to love.

But what he does off the ice is none of my concern. I just want to play good hockey with him.

When I reach the restaurant where we agreed to meet, I look around and find a place to park.

Lennox is out by the entrance and gives me a wave when he sees me hopping out of my Rover.

I wave back and walk over to him.

"Hey, good to meet you," he says as we shake hands. "Welcome to the team."

"Thanks," I reply. "I'm looking forward to playing here. Sometimes there's nothing like a good fresh start to get things going."

"I agree," he says. "And speaking of getting things going, I'd like to talk to you about something. But first"—he motions to the door—"let's go inside and grab a table."

I nod. "Sounds good to me."

I'm curious to hear what he has on his mind that he wants to talk about with me.

I guess I'll find out soon enough.

Several minutes later, we're seated at a private booth, not a table, which is even better. We're at the back of the restaurant, where it's relatively quiet. We already ordered and chose the same thing—grilled chicken entrées with sides of sautéed spinach.

Our iced teas arrive, and when the waitress walks away, I pull my glass closer and ask Lennox, "So, what did you want to talk about?"

He takes a quick sip of his drink, then sets the glass down on the table. "I don't know if you've heard yet," he says, "but the guy who plays on my line at left wing just broke his arm this past weekend mountain climbing. A rock gave way, and even though he was secured, he fell some distance and bashed up his arm pretty good."

"Holy hell!" I exclaim, genuinely shocked because I hadn't heard about this. "That sucks. Is he okay otherwise?"

"He is," Lennox tells me. "But he's going to be out for a long while. In fact, considering all the surgeries ahead of him, I wouldn't be surprised if he misses the whole season."

I wince. "Man, that's awful."

"It is, but..." Lennox raises a dark brow. "This is where you come in, my friend."

I can't help but feel a building excitement as I venture to ask, "You want me up on your line at left wing?"

He nods. "Yeah, I do. I say let's try it out. You're too good for the second line, Easton. I've watched footage of you from last season with the Thunder, and you have some great moves."

"Thanks," I say.

"Anyway." He sighs. "Training camp starts this Thursday. If Coach goes for it, and I think he will, let's give it a go. What do you say?"

Damn, this is the opportunity I've been waiting for—a chance to play on the top line of a team.

"I'm in," I assure him. "Let's do this."

"Cool."

Our entrées arrive, so we pause the conversation so we can dig in. Everything is delicious, and once we're done, I lean back and stretch.

"That was good," I state.

"It was," Lennox agrees.

He then eyes me curiously, prompting me to ask, "What?"

Chuckling, he says, "I heard you got married."

See, I knew this would come up.

But I'm ready.

Blowing out a breath, I confirm, "Yeah, I did. I met up with a girl I once knew a long time ago. We were great friends back in the day. Anyway, sparks flew, and what can I say?" I shrug. "We just decided to do something wild and spontaneous."

"I'd say," Lennox replies. "I also heard you hadn't even seen each other in years."

I don't know how that detail got out, but when you're in the public eye, it's amazing how many people come forward with what they know or have heard.

Since there's no point in lying, I tell him the truth. "Yeah, it had been a minute. But then it turned out that she was out looking for me at the same time I was looking for her. When we came together, just *bam*." I hit the table once for emphasis. "Fireworks, man. Fireworks."

Okay, that's all mostly true. Maybe not the fireworks part, as it's not like we ended up in bed. But there was something there. Still is. I felt that attraction to Claire that's always been there as soon as I saw her that day.

"Damn," Lennox says, shaking his head. "I hope I find someone like that someday. But for now…" He winks. "I'm content with playing the field."

I laugh, and now it's my turn to say, "Yeah, I've heard."

He's nonplussed. "I'm sure you have, man. I'm sure you have."

I'm learning that if there's one thing about this Lennox Foley dude, he's unapologetic for who he is.

Hey, I like that.

He's as real as they get.

I have a feeling he and I are going to become good friends.

Now if only our connection translates onto the ice in the same way, we'll be more than set up to win.

And that is the goal.

Chapter

TEN

CLAIRE

"**S**o, lunch with your teammate went well?" I ask.

"It was fantastic, Claire," Easton replies animatedly. "Lennox seems like a decent dude. We really connected, but the best part is…" He pauses for effect. "Are you ready for it?"

"Uh-huh." I nod, twisting to face him, his excitement palpable and contagious. I can't wait to hear what he has to say.

It's evening, and we're out by the infinity pool facing the mountains as we watch the sun set, which is stunning, by the way.

Sitting here, side by side in nice, comfy cushioned loungers, has become our nightly ritual. It gives us a chance to enjoy how beautiful it is up here in Cave Creek while catching each other up on how our day went.

Good God, we may not be hitched for real, but we're already acting like an old married couple.

And you know what?

I like it.

Easton continues, his eyes meeting and holding mine. "So, get this. Lennox wants me up on the top line with him. Claire, the top fucking line!"

"Oh my God!" I exclaim, pumped for him. "No way."

There's true happiness in his blues as he confirms, "Yeah, the top line. Can you believe it? If it works out, this will be a dream come true for me."

"You deserve it," I tell him.

He does too. Easton works so hard on being the best he can be. He's been getting in ice time down at the arena even though it's not even required yet.

He's also been working with a conditioning coach. The mornings he's not on the ice, he's out running the trails around our house and spending extra time in the team weight room.

It's paying off. His muscles are bigger than ever, and he's looking so lean and cut. I try not to stare too much, as I don't want to get caught.

But God, his body!

Yeah, my fake husband is freaking hot, hot, hot.

But he's my friend first and foremost. I'd never make a move or encourage him to make one. What we have, and how we picked right up where we left off all those years ago, is just too special to screw it up with something that may or may not work.

Besides—and I keep reminding myself of this—Easton only married me as a favor and to fulfill a long-ago promise. It's not like he fell in love with me.

But what if he does?

Would that be so bad?

Stop, I command myself.

Sometimes I have these crazy thoughts, but they really need to come to an end. He and I are just freaking friends, and that's never going to change.

If it was going to, it would've by now, right?

I sigh heavily, and Easton's brow creases. "Hey, what's wrong?" he asks. "You look sad all of a sudden."

It's great that he's so observant, until it's not.

Like now.

"No, no, it's nothing." I wave my hand around. "I'm not sad. I was just lost in thought, that's all."

He cocks his head. "Are you sure you're okay? If you need to talk about something, Claire, you know I'm always here to listen."

Does he have to be so sweet all of the time?

"I know," I reply with a smile. "I appreciate that too. I promise, if there's something ever truly bugging me, you'll be the first to know."

"All right," he says. "I better be."

The way the setting sun is illuminating his features right now, he just looks so gorgeous.

Ugh!

I need to move around or something. I clearly have a lot of pent-up energy tonight, and it's making me think ridiculous things.

Sitting up straight in my lounger and planting my sneakered feet on either side of it, I say to Easton, "Do you want to take a walk on the trails? Kind of like we used to do at sunset?"

He nods and leans forward. "Yeah, sure, that sounds nice."

Thank God.

We take our walk through the trails around the house, where we joke around and laugh. It really is like old times.

That's why I need to do what I used to do all those years ago when thoughts of Easton would turn romantic—ignore them and bury them deep, deep inside.

Three weeks pass, and I'm back on track with keeping those pesky feelings for Easton from percolating up.

Well, for the most part, they're at bay.

How weird is it, though, that you have to keep yourself from having lusty thoughts about your own husband?

What a strange life I lead.

But it's the path I've chosen.

I roll my eyes at my wandering mind, as I should be concentrating on the game Madison and I are at right now.

Why am I always overthinking things?

I let out a big, frustrated huff, and Madison asks, "What's wrong?"

Uh-oh, better come up with something fast.

I motion to the ice and say, "Er, uh… I was just thinking how that pass from Easton to Lennox should have resulted in a goal."

"Well, it wasn't Lennox's fault," Madison replies, and I notice how quick she is to defend him. "The puck just kind of skipped off his stick. It happens, you know?"

"Yes, I know," I say. "It's just that hockey can be so frustrating sometimes."

"It can be," Madison agrees before returning her attention to the ice, where there's now a face-off in front of us.

We win it handily and play resumes.

This is the first game of the regular season for the Bears, and Easton got us front row tickets right up on the glass.

He said I had to come see him play, as he did indeed win the coveted spot on the top line.

I'm so proud of and happy for him, so I told him of course I'd come to the game. I wouldn't miss it for the world.

So here I am.

It's been fun too.

Easton and Lennox, and their guy at right wing, Shane Thoma, have fantastic chemistry. It was evident at training camp, and it's continuing tonight into the regular season.

Even though the last play didn't pan out, their line has done really well, scoring two goals already—one from Easton and one from Lennox.

The Bears are playing the Colorado Avalanche, which makes this an important game since they're division rivals.

The score is currently 2-0, which is great, especially since it's been kind of an open contest. Luckily, our goaltender has been beyond amazing. Still, we need to shut things down in the third and tighten up defensively to hold our slim lead.

It's the second period now, but time is winding down. In fact, there are only nine seconds left.

9-8-7-6-5-4-3-2-1, and the buzzer sounds.

The players leave the ice and a bunch of folks around us stand up, readying to go get food or drinks or head to the restrooms.

Madison and I decide to just remain in our seats during intermission so we can sit and talk.

Leaning back, I ask her, "Are you having a good time?"

Though she's been a hockey fan for a while now, this is her first in-person game. I told Easton that I definitely wanted to bring her to this matchup. She needs to see hockey in person.

"Hell yeah," my friend replies as she nods excitedly, her soft blonde curls bouncing. "I've always liked hockey, but being at a game is, like, next-level. You were so right."

"It is amazing," I agree. "So much more fun than watching it on TV."

"Definitely," she replies. "I hope we can come to more games."

"Pfft," I snort. "Are you kidding? Easton can get us tickets to any game we want to go to."

"Hmmm, I guess that's one of the perks of being married to a hockey player, huh?"

I shrug, and she narrows her green eyes at me. "What?" I ask.

"I was just thinking again about how I told you Easton was my client for that big house up in Cave Creek. But you never said a word that day about how you knew him. Annnd," she goes on, "then you freaking run off and marry the dude. I'm never going to forgive you, by the way, for not having me as your maid of honor."

"Oh, please." I roll my eyes at her. "Since when do you get into weddings?"

Madison is not the most romantic person. She's actually a "love 'em and leave 'em" kind of gal. She's a bit of a heartbreaker, that one.

"I guess you're right," she admits. And then she waggles her brows. "But I could get into playing pretend wedding night with that hot linemate of Easton's."

Oooh, now I'm curious.

"Wait, who?' I ask. "Do you mean Lennox or Shane?"

"Lennox," she replies. "Maybe you or Easton can arrange for

us to meet sometime."

Aha, now I know why she was defending him earlier.

But I have to warn her, "He's a real player, Madison. And I don't mean just on the ice."

"Eh." She shrugs. "Who cares? I'm kind of a player myself."

This is true.

Still, though, I'm reticent to set my friend up for potential heartbreak, especially with Easton's linemate. It could cause all kinds of trouble if it doesn't end well.

I'm thankful the third period is about to start. People are returning to their seats, and Madison and I have to stand several times to let them down the row. All the ups and downs put an end to any further talk of helping her hook up in any way with Lennox.

I mean, come on, I have enough on my plate with playing my role of pretend wife. I don't need to add "for-real matchmaker" to my résumé.

Chapter

ELEVEN

EASTON

We win the first game of the season, and, man, it feels great. Not only do we earn two points, but we do it against a division rival. That makes the victory that much sweeter.

But what's even better is that Claire was there the whole time watching me. It reminded me of old times when she would come to my high school games.

That's why I did the same thing I used to do when she was in the front row at a rink. I skated by during some downtimes, smiled at her, and tapped the glass with my stick.

Claire grinned back each time and even blew me a kiss once. I know that was for show, but damn if it didn't make my heart soar.

Speaking of kisses, I keep thinking a lot more about what

it would be like to kiss Claire. And I don't mean a chaste peck like the one I gave her at our wedding. I'm talking a real fucking kiss, one filled with passion and longing—the same passion and longing I keep tamping down.

I better keep doing that, though, as we have a fancy event to attend tonight.

A bunch of the Bears players, including me, have been invited to a formal dinner and auction for an animal rescue charity that our team supports.

There will be a lot of donors in attendance, and they love seeing the players in person.

I'm almost ready to go.

I have on my nicest black tux, a white shirt, and shiny black shoes. I just need Claire to make sure my bow tie is even and straight. It looks fine as far as I can tell from the reflection in the mirror on the inside of my walk-in closet door, but I want her to double-check.

After leaving my bedroom, I head down the hall to hers.

The door is ajar, but I don't just go in. I wouldn't want to catch her half-dressed.

Okay, maybe I would like that, but it wouldn't be appropriate.

So I knock lightly. "Is it all right if I come in?"

"Yes, yes!" she yells back, sounding frazzled. "I need your help anyway."

I open the door the whole way and step in, readying to go to her, but I'm stopped dead in my tracks.

Claire is standing in front of the mirror above her dresser, her back toward me. She has on a formfitting gold shimmery dress, and her shiny hair is pulled over one shoulder.

But what has me frozen in place is that her dress is unzipped all the way down to her ass, exposing her bare back.

Fuck, she clearly has on no bra.

And is that a thong I see?

Kill me now.

"Can you zip this thing up for me?" she asks, one hand reaching around her body in vain. "I can't quite reach."

"Um, uh, yeah." Swallowing hard, I stride over to her and place my hand on the zipper pull.

I look down, and—*oh hell*—she does have on a thong.

And her bare skin is so fucking smooth and sexy.

I'm so mesmerized that I hesitate, zipper pull in hand.

Claire murmurs, "Easton?"

Oops, busted.

I snap to it. "Yeah, I got it."

I begin to zip up her dress ever so slowly, and that's when our eyes meet in the mirror.

"You look fucking beautiful," I blurt out.

"Thank you," she replies softly.

Our eyes stay locked as I continue to zip up her dress. The whole while, I swear I see in her eyes what I know is in mine—lust.

I wish we were real husband and wife.

I'd be unzipping, not zipping, this thing so she could shimmy out of it and be left standing here in a thong. I'd lay her back on the bed that's only inches away from us and take that little undergarment off…with my teeth.

And then I'd make my way back up her body…to between her legs, where I'd—

"Easton?"

Oh shit.

"Yeah?"

With a knowing smile, she whispers, "I think it's zipped."

I look down. "Oh, yeah, it is." I release the pull and step back.

There's a stirring in my groin, but thank fuck, I'm not hard. Good thing, too, as when Claire turns around to face me, I catch her totally glancing down at my pants.

Her gaze lifts and reaches mine, and now it's my turn to give her a knowing smirk.

She bites her lip.

Then, looking away quickly, she says, "We better go."

I agree wholeheartedly. "Yeah, we better."

Damn, I can't wait till later tonight when I'm alone in my bed. I have a whole new fantasy to play out. And the best part is, I'm going to imagine Claire down here in her room, doing the same thing.

Based on how I just caught her looking at my junk, I think that could totally happen.

Fuck.

Shane, my linemate, tells another joke, and Claire, seated at the table between us, giggles.

I roll my eyes.

That one wasn't even that funny.

But what's really grating on my nerves is that this is Shane's eighth joke of the night—yeah, I've been counting—and Claire has laughed at each and every one of them.

At first, I thought she was just trying to be nice, but now I think she really finds his stupid jokes hilarious.

Okay, maybe I'm being harsh.

They're not that bad.

Shane does have some good one-liners that I've heard him chirp on the ice. Some of them are actually pure classics. He can be a funny guy.

I think I'm just jealous.

No, I know I am.

But I have no right to be.

Remember that, dude.

We're at the charity event, and dinner has just ended. Seated at the table with Claire and me is Shane, of course, as well as Lennox and some bimbo he brought with him.

Those last two have been busy whispering sweet nothings to each other all evening, so it's almost like they're not even here.

Fuck, I wish Shane had brought a date.

Now Claire's telling him a funny story about one of her former real estate colleagues, and he's eating it up.

I've heard the tale before, so I'm tuning it out. But not before I huff loudly.

I'm beyond thankful when an announcement is made that the auction is about to start.

Claire wraps up her story, and we all direct our attention to the stage at the front of the hotel ballroom we're in.

At first, a bunch of various gifts from sponsors are auctioned off.

Then it's time for things donated by the Bears to go up, most of which are signed sticks and pucks, as well as tickets to a slew of home games.

The final three items up for auction involve me and my teammates here at the table. They're all for special outings with the players on the top line.

I'm paying full attention now, as the last one is for going out to lunch with me. I'm curious to see who puts in the top bid on that one and wins.

It's been a good night for the rescue, but I hope these last auctions raise even more money for them. It's such a good cause.

First up in the final three auctions is a chance to skate for twenty minutes at the Glacier Dome with Lennox.

Bidding is fierce, and a middle-aged guy ends up winning that one.

Although he did all of the bidding, when Lennox goes up to the stage to shake his hand, the man sends up his son, who looks to be in his early teens, to accept the prize.

The kid is so excited that he starts crying.

It's sweet, and everyone is touched.

The next auction is for a tour of our facility with Shane as the guide.

An older lady wins that one. She seems a little flustered when she meets my teammate on the stage and has to shake his hand, but that's not entirely surprising, as Shane is a really good-looking guy.

Shit, now it's my turn.

Who will win lunch with me?

I'm the new guy on the team, so I don't expect a ton of bids to pour in. Fans just don't really know me yet.

But to my surprise, the bids start coming in at a respectable pace.

Claire glances over at me and gives me a reassuring smile.

Shit, now I feel bad that I've been so jealous tonight. I hope she hasn't noticed. But knowing Claire, she has.

I'll have to apologize later.

Oh hell, I just realized we have a winner.

I wasn't even paying attention, when that was my whole goal.

Damn it.

I get up and head to the stage to meet whoever the winner is.

To my surprise, I'm joined by a hot-ass chick with a platinum blonde bob. She's attractive and about my age, but what really stands out is how she's dressed. She's wearing a slinky, hot pink low-cut dress that leaves little to the imagination.

Wow.

Hey, I am still a guy.

And I'm not even really married.

I can look.

She shakes my hand and bats her long lashes at me.

I chuckle a little, shaking my head.

I tell her, "Congratulations," and that I'm looking forward to lunch.

She replies, "Oh, so am I, Easton, so am I."

Oh boy.

I return to the table, and holy shit—Claire looks beyond pissed.

"You okay?" I ask as I sit down next to her.

"Yes," she snaps, turning her head and sniffing. "I'm fine."

Oh my God, she's jealous, much like I was earlier. But she truly has nothing to worry about. Hot Girl may be smokin', but I'm not interested.

I do, however, allow myself a moment to enjoy the satisfaction that I'm not the only one who's been feeling pangs of jealousy, especially tonight.

The only thing perplexing is, if we're only friends, why are we feeling this way?

Chapter

TWELVE

CLAIRE

After the charity dinner and auction, I'm feeling all kinds of confused.

Why was I so jealous of that girl who won the lunch with Easton?

Why am I still irritated?

The "date" hasn't even happened yet.

But I dread it.

Why, though?

And why did I pay so much attention to Shane?

Not all of his jokes were that funny.

I guess I wanted to see if Easton would notice and get jealous.

I could tell that he did. I caught him rolling his eyes, and once he even let out an aggravated huff.

I really liked that.

But I shouldn't have.

That's why I'm glad that after a couple of additional home games following that dinner, the team went on the road for a bunch of away matches.

In fact, they're still gone.

Though I've missed Easton, we need this time apart to get back to what we are—good friends. The night of the dinner, when he came into my bedroom and zipped up my dress, we shared an unexpected lusty moment.

It was unplanned but so real.

I felt warmth emanating from him as he stood so close behind me, his hand on the pull of my zipper. He was clearly distracted by my bare back, so much so that he wouldn't even meet my gaze in the mirror as he began zipping me up—oh so slowly.

It was tortuous, and it was hot.

I was hot, my skin screaming for his touch.

When our eyes finally met in the mirror, I could see how much he wanted me.

Hell, I wanted him too.

But we can't ever act on an impulse. We have too much to lose. That's why I said his name, breaking him from whatever illicit thoughts were running through his mind.

Probably the same thoughts as mine, to be honest.

I gave him a knowing grin. But then he shot me one, too, when he caught me glancing down at his junk as I turned to face him.

Okay, I was curious to see if he was aroused.

I know I sure was.

But, again, we have to stop that.

We can't screw up this fake marriage, damn it!

Easton is only with me as a favor and fulfillment of a promise. It's all about the trust fund money. I need to remember that.

Speaking of those funds, while Easton has been away, I've been busy meeting with my financial advisers and attorneys. I've diversified my portfolio for maximum gains, and the charitable foundation we want to create for the children's hospital is just about set up.

My lawyers have been in talks with the Bears, and thankfully they're going to allow Easton to represent the foundation in his role as a professional hockey player. That will bring so much more visibility to our endeavor.

I can't believe how everything is working out.

But truly what I'm most pumped about is that the team is coming home today.

Easton will be back.

Yay!

Even though we've texted and talked over the past week and a half that he's been out of town, it's not the same. We've really just discussed my meetings and how our new charitable foundation is

73

coming along.

But damn it, I miss spending time with him.

We haven't mentioned it in our calls or texts, but after that charity dinner, we kind of avoided each other for the few days he was still here.

Then he left to go on the road.

I just want everything back to normal. I'm hoping we can return to our routine of sitting out by the pool and catching up, as well as taking walks.

Maybe we can even do one of those things tonight. It's after three, so Easton should be back any minute now.

That reminds me—I better check on the homemade lasagna I put in the oven a while ago. It's probably just about done.

Yep, I made us dinner.

I hope he likes it.

It's my mom's recipe, and I remember from the past that when he'd come over to have dinner with us, he especially loved my mom's lasagna. He said back then that it was "the best" he'd ever had.

High praise, and that's why I made it today. I also threw together a mixed green salad as an accompaniment.

Before I head to the kitchen, I pop into a downstairs powder room to make sure I look all right.

My hair is down, so I fluff it out. Then I straighten the teal knit shirt I have on and pick off a piece of lint from my faded jeans.

"Okay, all set," I murmur to my reflection. "Let's go check on that lasagna."

Turns out, it's ready, all cheesy and gooey on top, just like Easton always liked it.

With a big smile, I remove the cooking pan from the oven and place it on the counter.

Next, I put the salad bowl on the table, then turn to the refrigerator to grab a pitcher of iced tea.

Just in time, too, as I hear Easton coming in.

"Hey," I call out. "I'm in the kitchen."

A moment later, from the doorway, I hear a soft "Hey."

I spin around, pitcher in hand, but I don't immediately set it on the table.

It's just that *wow*—Easton looks *sooooo* good, leaning casually on the door frame, arms crossed, his dark blond hair a little mussed, and his blue eyes sparkling.

"I made dinner," I blurt out. Quickly, I slide the pitcher onto the table. "I hope you didn't eat already."

He shakes his head as he uncrosses his arms and pushes away from the frame.

Damn, even that little move is hot.

"I didn't," he says, stepping over to the table and picking out a cherry tomato from the salad. "I'm actually starving."

As he pops the morsel into his mouth, I say, "Good."

"What are we having?" he asks after he's swallowed. "Whatever it is, it smells fucking delicious."

I make a grand gesture to the counter. "Lasagna," I announce with a big grin.

His eyes widen. "No way."

Laughing, I nod. "Oh, yes. And…" I turn to pick up the potholders so I can grab the pan from the counter. Placing it on the table, I share, "It's my mom's recipe."

"Damn, woman." Easton plops down onto a chair. "I come home from a long trip, and you've made what used to be one of my favorite dinners? You are way too good to me."

I like that he just said all that.

And I like that he's pleased I made him dinner.

But that's okay.

These are things you do for your best friend, right?

I shrug nonchalantly as I take a seat across from him. "Eh, it was the least I could do to welcome you home. It's been a while."

"It has," he agrees. And then, his eyes meeting mine, he says softly, "This dinner is very much appreciated, Claire. Thank you."

In a voice just as soft, I tell him, "You're welcome, Easton."

We dig in then, and the man is instantly in heaven. Or so it looks from the expression on his face. I mean, his eyes are closed, and he's clearly savoring his first bite.

"Oh my God," he says, pointing to the square of lasagna on his plate with his fork. "This is better than your mom's. I'm not kidding. I don't know what you did, but this is just next-fucking-level."

I laugh and murmur a humble "Thanks," but inside I'm fist-pumping the air.

Yes, success!

I added more cheese than Mom usually does, but otherwise, it's the same recipe. Of course, Easton loves cheese, so it makes sense that he'd like mine better. In any case, I'm happy this dinner is a hit.

"I'll have to cook us more things," I tell him.

"I would love that," he replies. But then, turning serious, he says, "Only if you really want to, though."

I assure him, "Don't worry, I only cook if I really feel like it."

"Good." He nods approvingly, then says, "Maybe I can make something for you sometime too. I'm not the greatest in the kitchen, but I can grill up some mean-ass steaks."

I don't know what exactly "mean-ass" steaks are, but I assume they're good, so I laugh and say, "Sounds like a deal."

As we work on our meals, conversation continues to flow freely. Easton tells me all about his away games.

I listen with rapt attention, even though I watched them all. It's still fun to hear his perspective and the behind-the-scenes scoop.

He shares with me at one point that Lennox hooked up with an old girlfriend in Vancouver.

I ask, "Do you think anything will come of it?"

He chortles, "No. That's just typical Lennox behavior. She was there and willing, so..."

I roll my eyes. "Good God, that just confirms it. I am never introducing him to Madison."

I told Easton that my friend has the hots for Lennox, but he agreed with me—setting them up is probably a bad idea.

"Yeah," he says, hacking off another hunk of lasagna with the side of his fork. "I wouldn't get those two together."

After dinner, we clean up the kitchen. We make a good team, with him handing me the dishes and me loading them into the dishwasher.

Once we're finished, we both agree we're up for a walk to burn off some of the calories and carbs from our rich meal.

But first we change out our shoes—my strappy sandals and his loafers—for sturdy hiking boots.

"Are you ready?" Easton asks as we meet back up in the entry hall.

"Yep," I confirm.

He pops open the front door, and I follow my husband—*God, it still feels so weird thinking that*—outside.

Chapter

THIRTEEN

EASTON

What I told Claire was the truth—her lasagna dinner was fucking delicious. And yes, it requires an expletive, as it was that fantastic. "Next-level" was truly an understatement.

I'm glad we're now taking a walk on the trails around the house. I really don't care about working off calories and carbs; I just want to spend more time with Claire.

I fucking missed her.

Yes, again, the expletive is required.

Things were a little weird with us after the charity dinner, but we seem to be back on track. We're laughing and joking as we wind down the desert path, just like old times.

And that makes me think of something, prompting me to say,

"Hey, you know what we need to do?"

This part of the trail is wide enough that Claire is walking next to me.

Glancing over, she asks, "What's that?"

"We need to find a Stan."

She looks confused for a beat, but then it hits her, and she exclaims, "Oh my God, I forgot all about him! Yes, we definitely need to find us one."

Stan was a big ole saguaro cactus located on one of the trails in our neighborhood area where we used to walk. One of his arms was angled in such a way that he looked like he was waving.

So we named him Stan.

We passed by him and sat next to him at the picnic table nearby so many times over the years that he became like an old friend.

So we embark on a mission now, searching for a new Stan. Every twist and turn, and even on the straightaways along the trail, Claire and I scour the area, searching for a suitable new "friend."

But we come up with nothing.

The sun is setting, and it'll be dark soon, so, with a sigh, I say, "We better head back. We can look around another day."

"Yeah." Claire blows out a breath. "I guess we should go home."

We traverse the same trails on our return until we're not far from the house.

And that's when an idea pops into my head.

There's a fork in the path up ahead, so pointing to the right side of it, I say, "Do you want to take that trail back instead of the one we came down?"

Claire knows I'm thinking this could be a last-ditch effort to find our new Stan tonight.

She nods excitedly and says, "Yes. Good idea. Our Stan could be down there."

"He could," I agree, feeling optimistic.

Once we start down our alternate route, I notice right away that it's much windier than the other trail, but the terrain is more open.

Navigating the twists and turns, we eventually reach a sharp L-bend.

Stopping and turning to face me, Claire says, "I think we've hit the final stretch. Guess this trail is a bust too."

I sigh. "Yeah, it looks that way."

And it does, until we hit the hard right angle of the bend, and lo and behold...

"Stan!" Claire exclaims.

"Holy fuck!" I start laughing as we walk up to a cactus that could be the original. "I can't believe we actually found one that looks so much like our old guy."

"Right?" Claire shakes her head in disbelief. "It's so close to the house too. It's like it was meant for us to live here."

"Shit, it really is," I concur.

It's unbelievable how fate or kismet or whatever brought us

back together in the first place. And now we even have a new Stan right on our property.

I tell Claire, "You know, this is close enough to the house that I can drag a picnic table back here. I mean, I'll have to buy one first, of course. But bottom line…" My eyes meet hers. "We can sit out here like we used to by our old Stan."

Smiling, she says, "I love that idea."

"Then consider it done."

With that decided, we also come to the conclusion that we should name this cactus New Stan, in honor and memory of the original one.

The short walk back to the house is an enjoyable one. We're both happy.

It seems the past and the present are coming together in such a way as to create a most promising future.

A future I am all in on.

Chapter

FOURTEEN

CLAIRE

Easton is at morning practice with the team, and I'm visiting my mom at her new house, which, of course, used to be my old place.

She hasn't made too many changes yet. At least nothing major. Except in the kitchen, where we're currently seated at a new wooden table, having coffee.

Guess Mom didn't like my sleek dark teakwood furniture. She's also replaced most of the southwestern motif I had going in the kitchen with a flowery one.

That's okay.

This is so Mom.

As I pick up my dainty rose-covered china cup to take a sip of coffee, I notice her peering over at me curiously.

"What?" I say, forgoing the drink and setting my cup down. "What's going on in your head? You have that look."

"What look would that be?" she asks innocently as she smoothes back her gray-streaked dark hair that's up in a neat bun.

"The look that tells me you're dying to ask me something," I reply.

"Oh, okay." She waves her hand around, acquiescing. "There's no sense in lying. You're right."

"So, what's the question?" I ask as I finally take a sip of coffee.

She really is dragging this out.

I realize why she was so hesitant when she blurts out, "When do you think you and Easton may have a baby?"

I almost spit out my coffee.

I was not expecting that.

After swallowing carefully, I clear my throat and say, "Wait, what? Are you serious? Where is this even coming from?"

She sniffs, as if my reaction is ridiculous. Then she says, "Well, you are married now."

"For only, like, a little over two months!" I exclaim.

Mom shrugs. "I got pregnant with you when your dad and I had only been married for six weeks."

I roll my eyes as I mumble, "And look how well that turned out."

"Claire!" My mom is aghast. "Despite the fact that your father and I got divorced, I have no regrets. Our time together wasn't all that bad. He was just more married to his work than to me. Besides…" She levels me with a smug look. "If it weren't for him, you wouldn't even be here."

Okay, she's got me there. And really, I have no room to judge. Look at my crazy situation.

With a sigh, I say, "I'm sorry. I didn't mean to sound flippant or make light of your past with Dad."

She accepts my apology, but truly, what am I even doing?

I can't believe I'm having an argument with my mom about having a baby. I'm not even really married. I mean, I am, but only technically. If only Mom knew the truth—it'd be kind of hard to get pregnant when you don't even sleep with your husband.

Though there are days I wish I did.

Stop.

You don't.

And you can't.

Not to mention, I'm certainly not in any way, shape, or form interested in getting pregnant. Not at this time in my life. Though, man, I bet Easton would make a great father. Not like mine. He'd be in his child's life more than once a year.

But some things can never be.

"Why do you suddenly look sad?" my mom asks as she reaches over and places her hand over mine.

I shake my head. "It's nothing."

Patting my hand, she says, "I'm sorry, Claire. I shouldn't have brought up the subject. Having a child is your and Easton's decision to make, not mine. I'm sure when you guys feel the time is right, it'll happen."

Yeah, that time will never come, Mom.

I can't say that, of course, so I just nod in agreement.

Thankfully, the subject is dropped. Mom pivots, and we talk about how both of us are settling into our new homes. I also share that Madison and I are going to the Phoenix Bears game tonight.

"Ooh," Mom coos. "That should be fun. They're playing Edmonton, right?"

My eyes widen. "Whoa, Mom, they sure are. I'm impressed. Since when did you start paying attention to the Bears' schedule?"

After taking a small sip of coffee, she states proudly, "Since my daughter happened to marry one of their players."

I laugh. "Touché, Mom. Touché."

I stay at my mom's for a while longer, and then I head back to my house.

When I arrive, everything is quiet. I assume Easton is taking his usual routine before-game nap.

I don't want to bother him, so I decide to sit out on the back patio. It's not overly hot today since it's early November, but I still opt to take a seat at the table with the big umbrella shading the sun.

Once I'm settled, I notice I have a perfect view of where the trailhead that leads to Stan begins. It reminds me that I've been meaning to take a picture of that cactus. I have a few shots of the old Stan on my phone, but the new one has yet to be immortalized on my camera roll.

Leaning forward and slipping my phone out of my back pocket, I stand and then make my way over to the trailhead, where I embark down the windy path. Within a few minutes, I reach Stan.

I skid to a halt.

But for a good reason—there's a small wooden picnic table by our new friend. It's roughly the same size as the one that used to be next to the old Stan, but this one is in better shape. It's not sun bleached or worn.

Smiling, I murmur, "Easton sure didn't waste any time putting this thing back here."

I'm touched and also pleased.

This means we can sit and chill, just like we used to on the old neighborhood trail.

I take a few pictures of Stan from different angles, some including the picnic table.

But all I keep thinking the whole time is what a sweet husband I have.

Chapter

FIFTEEN

EASTON

"**F**uck!" I grind out as I'm checked into the boards—*hard*—by an Edmonton player.

We're on the ice right where Claire and Madison are seated, and as the glass reverberates, they both jump back.

Yeah, they're in the front row again. They really do like these close-to-the-action seats.

That's fine with me. I love seeing Claire during the game.

I glance at her now and notice that her hand is over her heart. There's also concern for my safety on her face.

I'm fine, just a little pissed that I didn't avoid that check.

Still, before I skate away, I turn back and give her a reassuring wink.

It's going to take a lot more than a punishing check to take me out of this game.

And what a game it's been. There's been loads of offense, which the fans always love. What they're enjoying even more is that we're currently up 6-5.

I can take credit for one of those goals.

Oh, and an assist as well.

Yeah, it's been a good night.

But we still have three minutes and twenty-two seconds left to play. Anything can happen. That's why we need to put this thing away with an "insurance" goal.

There's a TV time-out, so Coach waves us over to the bench to discuss strategy. He informs us that we, the top line, will stay out for one more shift.

We lean on our sticks and watch intently as he draws up a play on his dry-erase board.

The face-off will be in the opponent's zone, so if Lennox wins the draw, which he should, he'll shoot the puck straight to me.

I'll hopefully find a clear lane to get it on the net, but if not, I'll pass it to Shane or back to Lennox. Coach doesn't want the defensive guys getting overly involved, like pinching, as the last thing we need is for Edmonton to get a breakaway down the ice.

They're just too good and loaded with talent.

The time-out ends, and we get into position for the face-off. Even though we're up by one, my heart is racing. We need to score one more goal for me to feel good about our chances. I'd like to be the hero tonight, especially since Claire is in the stands.

Why does everything always come back to her?

I don't know, and there's no time to think about it now, as the ref just dropped the puck.

Lennox wins the draw cleanly and shoots the puck to me, just as planned.

Annnd I have a clear lane to the net.

What a break!

I shoot the puck, and it fucking goes in.

Yes!

The play worked out exactly as drawn up. That doesn't always happen, so we're extra exuberant in our celebration on the ice.

So are the fans.

They're going wild.

I feel like a million bucks. We have this game in the bag now. No way can Edmonton score two goals in the short amount of time that's left, especially if we tighten up defensively.

We do exactly that, and sure enough, even though they pull their goalie for the duration, they can't get anything past our netminder.

Time runs out, and we win the game.

I'm awarded the first star of the night. Claire is there to watch me skate out and lift my stick to the crowd.

As I skate by her, she gives me a big thumbs-up, and then claps excitedly.

Damn, I think she's more amped than I am. Just like in my high school hockey days—she was always my biggest cheerleader.

Back in the locker room, the vibe is high. We're all laughing and talking, and there's music on in the background.

Some of the guys are going out to grab a late dinner, but I'm too pumped to eat. Besides, I had a bigger pregame meal than usual, so I'm not really hungry.

Though maybe my real reason for skipping the dinner is that I just want to go home and see Claire.

Whatever the case, that's exactly what I do.

But when I arrive home, I find the house is quiet.

I'm let down. Claire may have gone to bed. Or what if she stopped somewhere with Madison? Her friend was driving tonight, so the fact that I noticed Claire's car in the garage when I pulled in is of no significance.

Disappointed, I drop my key fob onto the kitchen counter and head to the front of the house.

That's when I hear sounds coming from the living room; clearly it's the TV.

Awesome.

Claire is home after all.

I make a little noise out in the entry hall so I don't startle her. Then I lean on the door frame and clear my throat.

Claire twists around on the sofa. "Hey," she says with a smile.

"Hey back at you." I go in and take a seat next to her. Not too close, but not too far away either. "Whatcha watching?" I ask.

"Nothing really," she says as she blows out a breath. "I was just flipping through the channels. Why? Do you want to talk?"

"Sure."

Claire turns off the TV, then leans back on the arm of the sofa. As she pulls her legs up under her, I notice she has on the most vibrant purple fuzzy socks I think I've ever seen.

They match what she wore to the game and still has on—black leggings and a black-and-violet Bears hoodie—but damn, they are bright.

Pointing to her feet, I tease, "Wow, those things sure stand out."

"Heyyy," she protests. "I wore these to go with the hoodie."

"Well, they do, for the most part. But, man, I hope you didn't blind anyone."

"Ha ha." She lifts the throw pillow that's wedged between us and playfully smacks my jean-clad leg with it. "I had boots on over these, so shut up."

I hold up my hands. "Okay, okay. Since you're bringing out the big artillery"—I nod to the pillow, still in her grasp—"I give up."

She drops her weapon, which lands between us, as she murmurs, "Wise choice."

Looking at each other, we both start laughing. Having goofy fun like this is just so us. It always was, and I'm glad it still is.

"On a serious note, though," Claire says, "what about that game?"

"Right?" I nod. "It was amazing, wasn't it?"

She straightens one leg and, kicking the pillow out of the way, nudges me with her purple-sock-covered foot. "*You* were amazing," she amends.

I give her a humble smile. "Thanks."

We talk a little about the game, and I share with her, "Man, I'm still feeling pumped."

"I bet," she replies. And then she adds, "To be honest, I'm feeling kind of wound up myself."

Raising a brow, I throw out, "We could go somewhere if you want. You know, to expend all this excess energy."

She shrugs. "I don't know. It's getting kind of late. I think most places are closed or are closing."

"Yeah, you're probably right," I agree.

I'm actually glad she doesn't want to leave the house. I don't even really know what I was going to suggest. Go to a bar, a club? That's really not our scene.

"Hey, I have an idea," Claire says. "It's something we used to do in the past. But it might sound silly now. I don't know. Then again…" She shrugs. "Maybe it's not *too* silly."

My curiosity is piqued, as I have no clue what she may be thinking.

Twisting to face her more fully, I ask, "What's your idea?"

Smiling brightly, she says, "I think we should put on some music and dance."

"Dance?" I question.

"Yes, dance."

Suddenly, in a whoosh of memories, it all comes back to me. Claire and I used to listen to music and dance like wild fools. It was the most fun ever back then.

Maybe it could be again?

Now I'm smiling, and Claire says, "You remember, don't you?"

I nod. "I do."

"So, what do you think?"

I hold out my hand. "Hell yeah, girl. I love it. Let's dance."

Chapter

SIXTEEN

CLAIRE

Easton and I dance and dance and dance. Oh, do we dance—to new stuff, eighties tunes, nineties grunge, and a bunch of songs we used to rock out to ten years ago.

Finally, exhausted and hot, even though I lost the hoodie a while ago, leaving me in a thin T-shirt and leggings, I plop down on the sofa.

Slouching down till my head's resting on the back, I declare, "That's it. I'm done. I think I've burned off ten thousand calories in the past couple hours."

Laughing, Easton lowers the volume on the portable speaker we've been using and sits down next to me, slouching in the same way.

Again, though, that damn throw pillow is between us.

How did it even get back up here anyway?

Oh yeah, we almost tripped over it when we started jamming, and I tossed it onto the sofa.

"If you burned ten thousand," he says, "I think I did twenty."

I nod. "Probably. Your air guitar was pretty wild, especially when you jumped up on the coffee table."

"Hey," he replies, shrugging, "you got to give the masses a good show."

I laugh, as it was almost like we were putting on a concert. Once we moved the coffee table and two chairs out of the way, we had a lot of room to work with for our performances.

And we had a bunch of song choices.

We connected Easton's iPhone to the speaker first. And when we ran out of tunes we liked on his, we synced mine.

"That was a lot of fun," I say softly.

"Just like old times," Easton replies.

"For sure."

He smiles over at me, and for a beat, I'm lost in his blues, leading me to blurt out, "I don't know if I've ever told you this, but you have the coolest color eyes."

"Thanks," he says, chuckling. "But you know what? I kind of like yours too."

"Nah." I wave my hand around. "Mine are old boring hazel. You have nice icy light blue."

Sitting up straight, he declares with passion, "No way. Your eyes are not boring at all. There are little flecks of gold and green in them. They're super pretty. Claire."

I bite my lip.

Wow, I had no idea Easton ever really paid that much attention or that he felt so passionately about my eyes.

But I am flattered, so I murmur a quiet "Thanks."

He flops back against the sofa, and this time he closes his eyes. "Claire," he breathes.

"What?"

"Nothing." He opens his eyes and turns his head toward me.

"Oh, come on," I press. "You're clearly thinking about something."

"All right. What the hell." Looking up at the ceiling, he runs a hand down his face. Then he says, "Is there anything about our past that you regret?"

Okay, we're moving into serious talk here.

But I'm up for it. There are things I want to share with Easton, just thoughts about all those years ago. Like things I think he should know.

I don't plan to divulge everything tonight, but there is something I've been meaning to tell him about for a while now.

"I have some regrets," I reply honestly. "But probably one in particular that weighs on me."

Looking over at me with deep interest, he asks, "What's the

one that weighs on you the most?"

"Nope. No way." I shake my head. "You brought it up. You go first."

"Okay." He blows out a breath. "Here goes one—I regret that I never asked you out back then."

Holy crap!

Softly, I say, "I didn't know you ever felt that way about me."

Chuckling, he gestures over to me. "Come on, Claire. Look at yourself. You're beautiful, and you always were. It would have been weird if it had never crossed my mind."

Ahh, so he was attracted to me.

But that was back then, I remind myself. *Not now.*

Though could it still be?

"Claire?"

Easton's voice breaks me from my reveries. "Yeah?"

"What's your big regret?" he asks.

Oh boy, now I wish I'd never said that I have one.

But I can't back out now.

"Uhhh," I begin, sitting up straight and crossing my arms. "It kind of fits in with yours in a way."

He leans forward as well. "It does?"

"Yeah." I nod. "It definitely does."

"So, spill it, girl."

Oh hell.

"All right." I scrunch up my face and say in a rush of words, "I wish you had been my first."

"First?" He looks confused. But then he gets it. "Ohhh... Wow, really?"

"Yeah, really."

He winces. "Was it that bad?"

I nod. "It sucked."

"Damn, I'm sorry. But to be honest, I wasn't that good back then. I can't say it would have been much better."

I laugh. "I'm sure it would have." But then I realize something about what he just said, and my eyes widen. "Wait a gosh-darn minute. You were doing it back then when we were seventeen? With who? Not that Lori so-and-so chick?"

Why do I feel a spike of jealousy?

And why am I relieved when, chuckling, he says, "No, not back then. And I never would have done it with Lori whatever, anyway. She was so not my type."

"Well, that's good to hear," I say. "You do know she had a huge crush on you, though, right?"

He shakes his head. "No, I never knew that. Still, it wouldn't have changed anything. In fact, I didn't have sex until my first month of college. And about me not being that good from the start, I was just saying it took me a few times to get...you know... skilled."

My face warms, and, aww, he's blushing too.

"We are so weird," I say to lighten the mood.

He laughs. "Yeah, but that's why we make such good friends."

See, he views you as just his friend.

Stop with the dreamy thoughts.

Standing, he holds out his hand. "Ready to go to bed?"

With you, yes, my mind says.

My body agrees.

Good thing my mouth is in control, as I take his hand and reply, "Yeah, I'm exhausted."

"Same," he says as he helps me up.

He lets go of my hand, and we head upstairs, where we go our separate ways at the top.

A part of me would like to turn around and follow him into his bedroom.

But no, this is for the best.

I'm just sleepy and not thinking straight.

But still, I have to ask myself—is this one of those weird moments we have, or is that what I really want?

Well, it's not going to be answered tonight.

Chapter

SEVENTEEN

EASTON

A s tired as I am, I can't sleep. All I can think about is Claire sharing with me that she wishes I were her first.

I wish I had been too.

And I wish that she'd been mine.

True, I wasn't skilled like I am now. But despite what I told her, I know I would have made it better for her than the stupid douche who took her virginity. I'm sure of that because I cared about Claire back then.

"You still care about her now," I whisper out loud.

Yeah, yeah, I do.

But I don't want to fuck this up.

What we have is just so good. I can't lose her as my friend.

I lost her once.

I can't lose her again.

So things must remain as they are, no matter where my heart is pulling me.

This is my last thought before I doze off.

That weekend we have a home game on Friday, then a rare day off on Saturday. No practice, no drills, nothing. Because of the downtime, Lennox calls me to let me know he's decided to host a small gathering at his house this evening. There will be some appetizers and drinks and a chance to chill out before we go on the road for some games next week.

I tell him, "I'm in."

"What about Claire?" he asks.

"I'm sure she'll want to come too."

But after we disconnect, I figure I better make sure of that.

I seek her out, finding her in the laundry room.

After filling her in on the party details, I lean on the door frame and ask, "So, what do you think? Do you want to go?"

"I do, but…" she says, sighing as she takes out a bunch of towels from the dryer and plops them on the top. She then turns to face me. "Unfortunately, I already made plans with Madison to go see a movie with her tonight."

Ugh.

I am beyond disappointed.

But then I have an idea. "How about if you ask Madison if she'd like to come to the party with us instead?"

Claire laughs. "Oh, I'm sure she would. But I thought the idea was to keep her and Lennox far, far apart?"

"It was," I concede, chuckling. "And it still is. But how much can go wrong in one night? I mean, Lennox is hosting the party. It's not like he can sneak off with her and do God knows what."

"Ha," Claire barks out. "Clearly, you haven't seen Madison in action."

I sigh resignedly that Claire's sticking with her movie plans with her friend.

But then she holds up a hand and says, "With all that in mind, what's to say I can't keep her occupied? I'll just make sure we stick together at all times."

I raise a hopeful brow. "Does that mean you'll go?"

"Yeah, I will. And if she's up for joining us, which I'm sure she will be, I'll have Madison come over to the house. That way we can drive her over to Lennox's, meaning she'll have to leave when we do."

I nod approvingly. "Smart plan," I say. "I like it."

I start to walk away, but then Claire says, "Oh, crap. There is one more thing I forgot to tell you about."

Stepping back into the laundry room, I ask, "Yeah? What's

that?"

She leans back on the dryer. "I have a check for the children's hospital from the foundation we created, and I'm dropping it off on Monday afternoon. Anyway, they asked if you could come with me. They said it would be nice if we could stop in some of the rooms and visit the kids."

We're not leaving for our road trip until Tuesday, so I say, "Sure. I'd love that. I'll bring along some Bears merchandise too. I'll sign whatever we give out."

Excited, Claire replies, "That would be awesome."

"Then consider it done."

We high-five, and she says, "We make such a good team."

"We do," I agree. "We really fucking do."

Lennox's gathering is a blast. More players than he anticipated show up, and it becomes more of a bona fide full-on party.

That's okay; it's a good time.

And, so far, Claire and I have done a great job of keeping Lennox and Madison apart.

It hasn't been easy, though. Madison has on a slinky shimmery gold dress that is shockingly short, and I've caught Lennox checking her out a number of times.

That's no surprise. The girl looks good. But she's nowhere near as amazingly hot as Claire is.

Okay, maybe I'm biased. But fuck, my pretend wife is wearing a formfitting sparkly red dress and shiny black heels. Though her outfit isn't quite as short as Madison's, it still shows off her long, lean legs and hot-as-hell body to perfection.

Honestly, it's been hard for me to keep my eyes off of her.

And I'm not the only one.

Some of my teammates have taken notice of Claire too. But as soon as they catch me glaring at them, they quickly avert their eyes.

Yeah, smart move.

I know Claire's not really my wife in all aspects of the word, but damn, there are times like these when I wish she was.

Oh, who am I kidding?

It's not just times like these.

It's all the damn time these days.

I love her, of course, and have for years. But this is more. I think I've fallen in love with her.

No, I know I have.

I love Claire.

Man, I am so fucked.

Chapter

EIGHTEEN

CLAIRE

The party is fun. I'm having a good time. One thing I'm particularly enjoying is that I've caught Easton sneaking peeks at me so many times tonight.

But the way he's looking at me now from across the room is taking my breath away.

It's not just a look of lust this time.

It's…it's…

Could it be *love*?

And if it is, why does that make my heart fill with such joy?

Could I love him too?

Of course I do. He's my best friend.

But do I *really* love him?

Have I fallen in love with Easton?

"I think you know the answer to that," Madison says, jarring me back to reality and scaring the living daylights out of me.

Shit, did she just read my thoughts?

Or worse yet, did I say something out loud?

Fearing the latter, I ask her, "What are you talking about?"

She huffs, knowing I wasn't listening, then she says, "I was telling Shane here about how you and Easton are planning to visit the children's hospital soon, and he asked which day you're going."

Phew!

So she didn't read my thoughts. Nor did I unintentionally divulge them. But it is pretty sad that I didn't even realize Shane was standing next to her.

"Oh, hey." I give him a little wave. "I didn't even see you there."

Chuckling, he says, "Hi, Claire."

I catch Madison rolling her eyes, but I ignore her.

Focusing on Shane, I say, "We're going to the hospital on Monday."

"Ah, perfect. I was just telling Madison that I have some signed stuff that I'd love to donate. If you want, I can bring it to practice Monday morning and give it to Easton."

Wow, that is so nice of him.

"That would be wonderful," I reply. "Thank you."

"It's my pleasure," he says. "I'm happy to help."

Shane seems like a genuinely decent dude. Even now, he's not flirting with Madison or me. He's just talking to us like we're all old friends.

I'm glad he's the one who came over to chat and not Lennox. I don't have to worry about him hooking up with my friend.

The night continues to go well.

After Shane leaves, Easton comes over to spend some time with us. We all end up sitting on high-backed chairs in a little alcove on one side of the living room, where we drink some wine.

Okay, only I have wine, as Easton and Madison decline, opting instead for sparkling water.

Understandable, as Easton has to get us home, and Madison will need to drive from our house to her place.

I thought about asking her to just stay over, but how would I explain that I don't sleep in the same room, let alone the same bed, as my husband?

Yeah, that could be awkward.

Damn, this "marriage" gets more complicated as time goes by.

Sighing, I down a big gulp of wine, finishing off what's left in my glass.

Easton shoots me a funny look, and I ask, "What?"

I think he wants to say something like "Pace yourself," as this is my third glass and I really don't drink that much.

But he doesn't admonish me. He just shakes his head and murmurs, "Nothing."

As I turn away from him, one of his teammates walks by with

an open bottle, offering refills of wine, so I hold out my glass.

I feel my husband's eyes on me again, but this time I ignore him.

Can't a girl just have a good time?

Sheesh.

I mean, it's not like Madison's judging me.

Of course, she's too busy eyeing up Lennox, who's across the room.

He's looking at her too.

At one point, I even catch him winking at her.

Oh boy.

Easton must notice their interactions as well, seeing that he clears his throat and says, "We should probably get going soon."

"Definitely."

I down what's left in my glass.

I feel fine for the most part, until I stand up. "Oops." I almost stumble.

Easton cups my elbow, steadying me. "You okay?" he asks quietly.

"I'm fine," I declare, waving my empty glass around. "It's these damn high heels. It's a new pair, and I'm not used to them."

He scoffs, "Yeah, right. I'm sure it's just the shoes."

"Heyyy."

Gently prying my glass from my hand, Madison sets it on a side table, then hooks her arm with mine. "I got her," she tells

Easton.

"You two." I roll my eyes. "You're both so dramatic. I told you, I'm fine."

Even though they're overreacting, I allow Madison to keep her arm interlocked with mine as we leave the party.

Once we're in the Range Rover, I promptly take off my heels and toss them onto the back seat. Carefully, though, so as not to accidentally hit Madison, even though she's on the side behind Easton.

"There, that's better." I breathe out as I turn back around. "I won't be stumbling now."

I hear Madison snicker, and Easton just huffs.

"What?" I ask my friends.

But they say nothing.

It doesn't matter, as the drive home is kind of a blur.

The next thing I know, we're parked in the garage.

"Wow, that was fast," I remark.

"I think you dozed off," Madison says from the back.

I wave a hand and lean my head against the rest. "Whatever."

She gets out, as does Easton, but I decide that maybe I'll just stay right where I am. It's so comfy in the Rover.

When Easton comes around to the passenger side and pops open my door, I tell him, "I think I'll just sleep in here. These seats are so soft."

Chuckling, he says, "Yeah, I don't think so."

Before I can protest, he scoops me up with ease and lifts me out of the car.

"Hey," I grumble, but really I'm too tired to put up much of a fuss. Not to mention, I kind of like the way it feels to be cradled in Easton's strong arms, one of his hands on my back and, even better, the other touching one of my bare legs.

"So glad I wore a dress," I murmur.

Madison leans in and gives me a kiss on the head. "Hey, you get some sleep. I'll talk to you tomorrow, okay?"

"Yeah, tomorrow, good…"

I hear her and Easton exchange a few indecipherable words, probably about me, and then she leaves.

As the garage door powers down, I hold onto Easton, burying my head in his chest, as he walks us into the house.

"Mmmm," I murmur. "You're so warm, and you smell so good. What cologne are you wearing?"

"I'm not wearing any," he replies.

"Oh, wow. Must be the soap you used."

"Yeah, I guess."

As we reach the stairs, I run a hand over his pecs. "You're so freaking muscular, Easton. I like that," I groan. "God, I really, really like that. Have I ever told you this before?"

"I don't think so," he says. I feel him swallow hard, and then he rasps, "Let's just get you upstairs and into bed."

I snicker and lean my head back so I can look up at him. "My

111

bed or yours?" I slur.

Damn, I was trying to sound sexy.

Refusing to make eye contact, Easton says, "Yours, Claire."

"Are you going to join me?" I ask, giggling.

He huffs. "Claire, stop."

I smack his chest. "Aww, you're no fun."

Leaning my head back against him, mostly because I'm feeling dizzy now, I sigh.

Luckily, we make it to my room quickly.

Easton lays me down on my big bed, and I roll onto my side, where I wiggle up to my pillows.

But then I realize I still have on my dress.

"Can you help me out of this thing?" I ask as I sit up and start lifting the sequin hem.

"Claire, Claire, wait, hold up." Sounding panicked, Easton grabs my hand. "I really can't help you with this. Just stop for a minute. I'll grab you a T-shirt, and then I'll turn around while you change. I'm sure you can do it on your own."

I relent, directing him to where I keep my sleep tees in a drawer in my dresser.

After rummaging around in the drawer, he hands me a long light pink T-shirt with a V-neck and asks, "Is this one okay?"

"Perfect," I mumble.

He turns around, and I slip off my dress, tossing it on to the floor. I also ditch my bra, but I leave on my panties.

Tugging the tee down to where it falls about midthigh, then flopping onto my back because I have no more left in me to remain sitting, I say, "I'm decent. You can turn around now."

He does.

Quietly, he picks up my dress and bra. After placing them on a chair by the closet, he sits down on the edge of the bed.

"How do you feel?" he asks.

"Dizzy and headache-y." I close my eyes. "Ugh, why did I drink so much wine?"

Easton doesn't tell me, "I told you so," which he has every right to do.

He just remarks softly, "You were just letting loose and having a good time. There's nothing wrong with that."

"You tried to warn me with that look you gave me," I groan. "I should have listened."

Chuckling, he says, "You'll be fine. You need to just sleep it off."

"Still…" I roll onto my side, holding my head. "I'm never drinking wine ever again. It's not worth it."

"Do you want some aspirin?" he asks.

"Yes, please."

Easton heads into the en suite bathroom and returns with two aspirin and a tall glass of water.

He helps me sit up, and I swallow the pills and chase them down with a big gulp.

One brow raised, he asks, "Better?"

I wipe my mouth with the back of my hand and give him the glass. "Uh-huh."

"I'll leave the water here close to you," he says as he places it on the nightstand. "In case you get thirsty during the night."

I'm in the process of maneuvering to slip under the covers, so I mumble, "Thanks."

As I settle in, I can tell Easton is getting ready to leave.

But I don't want to be alone.

Peering up at him sadly, I ask, "Can you stay with me for a while? Like, maybe the whole night?"

He looks shocked. "You mean sleep in here?"

I nod and give him my saddest look. "Uh-huh."

He blows out a breath. "Um, okay, I guess, but..." Gesturing to his dress shirt and black slacks, he asks, "Do you mind if I run to my room and change into something more comfortable first?"

"Okay."

He walks to the door, and I double-check, "You're definitely coming back, right?"

With a smile, he tells me, "Of course."

"Promise?"

"I promise, Claire."

Closing my eyes, I let out a long, relaxed sigh. I know Easton will return. I can trust him. He always has my back, and he always keeps his promises.

Yeah, he married you, didn't he? I think as I drift off.

Chapter

NINETEEN

EASTON

I try to change out of my dress clothes and into dark lounge pants and a plain gray tee as quickly as I can.

I have to be fast. I forgot to ask Claire if she wants me to sleep with her in the bed—safely on one side and on top of the covers, of course—or if she prefers for me to stay on the chair that's over by the closet.

But when I return to her bedroom, she's fast asleep.

Now I need to make the decision on my own.

Shit, I hope I choose the right one.

I could always just go back to my own room, but I made a promise. And we all know how adamant I am about keeping my word.

So, will it be the chair or the bed?

The chair is kind of small. I won't get much sleep there. And Claire does look adorable all curled up on her side, one hand under the pillows. There's plenty of room next to her.

Aw, fuck it.

I decide to just lie down on the bed. But, as planned, I opt to stay on top of the covers. I don't want to overstep any boundaries here.

Though a huge part of me would love to wrap my arms around her, I don't. Again, this is new territory for us. And since Claire is impaired, I prefer to err on the side of caution.

So I just lie on my back, arms at my sides.

A surprisingly short while later, that's the way I fall asleep.

I wake up twice during the night. The first time is when Claire gets up to go to the en suite bathroom. I listen long enough to make sure she's not getting sick, which she isn't, and then I nod back off.

The second time I'm roused is when I feel Claire resting her hand on my chest.

That one makes me smile.

And then I'm back to dreamland.

The third time I wake up, it's morning.

The blinds are closed, but there's a little bit of light coming in, enough to see Claire's now on top of the covers with me.

Uh, and we're facing each other.

But that's not the end of it. Claire is snuggled in close to my chest, her hand clenching my tee. My arm is around her, holding her protectively.

I must've done that in my sleep.

I...don't...move.

I want to savor this moment.

I can't help but think this is how it should be every night. Too bad that's just a wish. Tonight I'll be back in my own bed down the hall, and Claire will be in here.

Even though I'm still as can be, Claire begins to stir.

Maybe she senses I'm awake.

In any case, I can tell when she wakes up by the way she sucks in a clearly surprised breath.

But she also doesn't move.

We just lie still, pretending like we're both asleep.

But then, out of the blue, I feel her press her nose into me and breathe in.

I take a chance and run my hand down to the small of her back.

She grips my T-shirt more tightly.

I breathe out.

She breathes in.

I breathe out.

She breathes in.

And then she murmurs, "Easton?"

"Yeah?"

She lets go of my shirt and scoots up.

I pull back my arm.

Still facing me, my head on one pillow and hers on another, and with a little more space between us now, she smiles at me and says, "Thank you for taking care of me and staying with me last night."

"Anytime," I reply.

She winces. "Ugh, hopefully you won't have to do this again any time soon. I don't plan to go overboard like that in the future."

I laugh. "I don't think anyone ever plans to go overboard, Claire. But if it ever happens again, I'll be here for you."

"Thank you," she murmurs. "I'll do the same for you too."

That's us, taking care of each other.

She sighs, and with my brow creasing in concern, I ask, "How do you feel now? Still pretty bad?"

"No." She shakes her head on the pillow. "Surprisingly, I'm okay."

"Good. The aspirin and water probably helped."

"I think so."

Man, I love how we're lying here in bed together and everything is just so relaxed and mellow. I was worried there'd be some awkwardness today, but that isn't the case.

Since all is good, I ask her if she'd like for me to make us breakfast. "That is," I qualify, "if your stomach feels up to it."

"Yeah." She touches her belly. "Breakfast would be great. I'm actually really hungry."

"Then let me go get things started."

I slide off the bed, and Claire, sitting up, tells me, "I think I'm going to go take a shower first. I feel kind of icky from drinking. But I promise I'll be quick."

"No problem." I reply, stretching and twisting to loosen up. "Eggs and bacon sound good?"

"Mmmm, sounds perfect." Then she adds, "Oh, and can we have toast? Lots of toast."

"Sure." I nod. "I'll make plenty."

I head down to the kitchen, leaving Claire to take her shower. I don't rush with getting everything together to allow her time to make it down.

And the timing turns out to be perfect. Claire walks into the kitchen just as I'm plating the eggs.

I look over at her long enough to see she has on black leggings and a violet-and-black Bears tee.

"Cute shirt," I say with a laugh.

I actually love when she wears my team's colors.

But I keep that one to myself.

"Thanks," she says as she takes a seat at the kitchen table, where I've already placed flatware and two tall glasses filled with orange juice. "I thought I'd show a little team spirit today."

"Hey, I'm cool with that." I pause, then say, "Oh, I forgot to ask you earlier, but I remembered you always loved your eggs over easy. Hope that's still the case."

"It is," she replies.

"Great." I add a couple of slices of crispy bacon to her plate, then set it on the table in front of her. "Here ya go. Enjoy."

"I think I will," she tells me. "This looks delicious."

And then I remember. "Crap, I forgot the toast."

After loading up the six-slice toaster, I grab a tub of butter and two different types of jelly from the fridge.

A few minutes later, Claire has her toast.

As do I.

With my own plate filled, I join her at the table.

As we eat breakfast, we talk about the party and how, despite Claire overindulging a bit, it was still a good time. We also give ourselves props for successfully keeping Madison and Lennox apart.

"Though, damn, did you see the looks they were giving each other?" Claire asks.

After taking a sip of juice, I set my glass back down on the table and nod. "I did. Keeping those two away from each other forever is going to be a challenge."

"It is," she agrees. "But if anyone can do it, we can."

I chuckle. "I think so too. We have so got this."

"And you know why, right?" she asks.

Curious, I raise a brow. "Why's that?"

Holding up her glass as if to make a toast, she states matter-of-factly, "Because we make a great team, Easton. I know we seem to say that a lot, but it's so damn true. We always did make a good pair, and we always will."

Hell, I'll toast to us any day.

Smiling and tapping my glass to hers, I say, "You got that right, babe. Every last word of it."

Chapter

TWENTY

CLAIRE

Yesterday was all about relaxation and fun. After Easton made that awesome breakfast, we hung out all day. We watched a movie on TV, took a walk around the area, and even spent some time sitting at the table by Stan.

But today is serious—we're at the children's hospital.

I'm wearing a simple gray sweater dress and tall boots, and Easton has on jeans and a Bears jersey with his number—14.

After we meet with hospital officials, where I hand over a big-ass check, we get to go see some of the kids.

And wow, the children we visit with, despite all the adversity and challenges in their lives, are truly a joy and an inspiration. They put into perspective what is really important in life.

To keep things light, though, we pass out lots of Bears merchandise, including the signed items Shane donated. Easton also autographs a bunch of jerseys and ball caps in person.

The kids love that. They ask him questions about hockey and what it's like to play on a professional team. Easton totally gets into it.

Damn, he is so good with kids.

My heart is warmed.

But isn't it always with him?

That man.

I can't help but smile.

Before we walk into the next room, he catches me grinning and asks, "What's up?"

I shake my head. "You're just amazing, that's all."

He laughs, then tells me, "Well, I think you're pretty awesome, too, Claire."

Our eyes meet, and we're about to have another one of those moments that keep popping up more and more.

But then the nurse taking us around breaks the spell when she says, "Before we go into Lydia's room, I have to warn you, she's a very prescient child. She sees things in people that most don't. Or can't. Good or bad, she's not afraid to tell you. She's what we call around here 'brutally honest.'"

I tease, "Okay, I'm a little nervous now, but I'm sure we'll be just fine."

"Oh, you will be," she assures us. "She's truly a doll."

We then go into the room.

Lydia is small and frail, but she greets us happily and with a big smile. "You're both so pretty," she says to me and Easton.

That makes him laugh.

Looks like she does just say what's on her mind. But so far, she's not too brutal.

We talk with her for a bit, and Easton gives her a signed jersey and a Bears ball cap.

She immediately discards her pink knit tassel hat onto the bed and replaces it with the violet Bears cap. "I love this," she gushes.

The nurse looks over at us and smiles. "Thank you," she mouthes.

It's about time to go, so we begin to say our goodbyes.

But as we turn to leave, Lydia asks, "You're married, right?"

Easton and I turn back around, and I say, "Yes, we are."

She frowns. "But you're keeping a big secret. And I don't understand why."

"Lydia," the nurse says sternly, "remember what we talked about, okay?"

I assure her, "It's fine."

The little girl then looks at me and says, "You love him very much, don't you? But he doesn't really know that, does he?"

Help.

It's clear she means "love him very much" in a romantic sense, not just friendship.

I can't even look at Easton.

And there's no time to anyway, as Lydia points to him and says, "And you love her just as much. But she doesn't know that either."

The nurse jumps in again. "Lydia, of course they love each other. They're married."

"Yeah, they are," this amazing child states matter-of-factly. "But they're also not."

"Okay, okay." The nurse ushers us out and issues an apology.

Damn, if she only knew. Lydia was spot-on with everything she said.

But does that mean Easton loves me in the same way?

Is he *in* love with me?

This is the question on my mind the whole drive home. I kind of want to discuss what Lydia said, but Easton doesn't bring her up. He talks about every other child we visited, but not her.

That leads me to believe that though little Lydia was right about our real-but-not-real marriage and my true feelings for Easton, she didn't read him correctly at all.

And that makes me so sad.

Chapter

TWENTY-ONE

EASTON

Oh my God, that kid. I wanted to disappear into the floor when Lydia said that I love Claire. I mean, of course she knows I love her. But she has no idea of the depths. Yeah, the truth is I am madly *in love* with her.

I wasn't sure, though, if Lydia was right about Claire loving me in the same way. So, on the way home, I was careful not to bring her up. Doing so would have required a discussion, and maybe even revealing our hearts.

Mine just couldn't take it if Claire were to laugh it all off.

So, nothing was resolved.

I'm beginning to think nothing ever will be. I believe Claire and I will continue to go on being great friends with a fake marriage.

And that's all.

Maybe it's for the best.

Yeah, keep lying to yourself, dude.

But now is not the time for these thoughts to be invading my head. We're in the middle of the first of three away games—this one is against the Los Angeles Kings—for fuck's sake.

Shane, nudging my shoulder, says, "Dude, come on. Get with it. We're up."

Shit, we sure are.

I hop over the boards with my linemates, making the switch just in time for me to intercept the puck at the blue line.

I skate the other way into the opponent's zone, with my linemates trailing me.

We get set up pretty quickly and begin passing the puck around like a finely oiled machine—me to Lennox, Lennox to Shane, then up to a defenseman, and then back to me.

I'm to the left of the net, but Shane is right in front of it. He's jockeying for position with one of the Kings' bigger players.

Shane looks to be winning that battle, so I take a chance and pass the puck to him.

He gets it, shoots, and scores.

Yes!

We're now up 4-1, and there are only a few minutes left in the third and final period.

We lock down defensively and win the game.

The locker room is fun and upbeat. Everyone is in a good mood. A bunch of the guys want to go out to a local club. They ask me to join them and let me know there's a private party room in the back where we can hang and not be bothered.

I generally don't attend these types of outings, but I'm in such a great mood that I say yes. Lennox and Shane are going, too, so it should be a fun time.

A couple of hours later, I'm proven right. My teammates and I are in that back room, playing cards, shooting pool, and listening to the music streaming in from out in the main club area.

We're all unwinding after a fantastic game.

I play a few rounds of poker and come away with a couple hundred bucks. It's all in good fun. I'm sure I'll lose it the next card game, probably the one we'll inevitably play on the flight to Seattle, the next city we're going to.

It's getting late, and we'll be heading back to the hotel soon, so when I see Lennox seated on a sofa in the rear of the room just relaxing, I stride over to hang with him.

Only problem is, as soon as I sit my ass down, some long-legged blonde in a blaring-red micro dress, who looks beyond tipsy, bumbles her way over and plops down on Lennox's lap.

"I wondered where you'd gone," she whines to him. "You left me out on the dance floor all alone."

Some of the guys have ventured out to the main part of the club to dance and mingle. I guess Lennox was out there while I was playing cards. Someone must've seen them together to have let her back here. Or maybe her drunken ass just snuck past the young employee manning the door. He has been on his phone a lot.

Lennox, placing a hand on her bare thigh in a placating manner, says, "Aw, baby, I didn't mean to do you like that. But the guys and I have to leave soon." He gives her a boyish shrug. "I can't miss my ride back to the hotel, you know?"

It's true, we will be taking off soon. We all took the hotel shuttle over and arranged for the driver to come back and get us by 1:00 a.m., which is in about fifteen minutes.

"I have an Uber coming," she counters in somewhat slurred words. "You could always just come home with me. I can drive you back to your hotel in the morning."

For as much as Lennox can be a player, I know he'd never take advantage of a girl who clearly has had too much to drink. I mean, the dude does have *some* morals.

"Not tonight," he tells her, patting her leg. "In fact, I think you should get up. Your Uber is probably waiting outside for you."

"Yeah." She sighs as she slides off his lap to the spot on the sofa in between us. "You're probably right."

I try to scoot farther away, and that's when she takes notice of me.

"Heyyy," she says, closing the small gap between us. "What about you? You're cute. What are you doing tonight?"

Uh-oh, we clearly have a puck bunny on our hands…and a drunken one at that.

"I'm married," I say to back her off.

"Aww." She purses her full lips into a pout. "Why are the good ones always taken?"

I ready to stand, sure that I've staved her off, but then the puck bunny chick throws her arms around me.

As I turn to say, "What the fuck?" she plants a big sloppy kiss on my lips.

Fuck.

I jerk away and stand up swiftly, but I swear I see a flash go off. There may have been one when she kissed me too. It's hard to tell, as a lot of the guys have been taking pictures with their phones all night long.

Still, double fuck.

Even though my teammates know it was nothing, I don't want that moment immortalized.

But what can I do?

Check everyone's phones and make them delete pictures?

I don't think so.

Sighing, I walk away, as I'm done with this shit. Lennox can make sure the girl gets out to her Uber. All I want to do right now is get the fuck out of this club and put an end to this night.

Chapter

TWENTY-TWO

CLAIRE

Easton is due to come home from the Bears' three-game road trip very late tonight. I'm kind of excited. No, I am excited. I can't help it—I always miss him when he's away.

I probably won't wait up, though. I'll just see him tomorrow.

But today should fly by, seeing as Madison is coming over to spend the afternoon.

In fact, the doorbell just rang.

I rush to the entry hall to let her in, greeting her with a big smile. But she doesn't look too happy.

"What's wrong?" I ask, my grin faltering.

"We have to talk," she replies as I step back and she walks in. Holding up her phone, she adds, "I need to show you something."

"Okay." I place my hand over my heart. "Good God, you're scaring me."

Madison blows out a breath. "I'm sorry. It's not life-and-death, so don't be scared. But it is bad. I mean, maybe it looks worse than it is. I don't know." She shrugs. "In any case, it's something I think you should see. And it's better if I show it to you as opposed to you seeing it online or something."

"Okay, this is weird," I mutter.

"It is," she agrees. "You'll see."

I suggest we head into the living room. I want to be sitting down when I view this something "weird" that has my friend so concerned.

Once we're seated on the sofa, Madison says, "So, it's about Easton."

What could she know about him that I don't? We've texted and talked several times while he's been away, and he's not once mentioned anything out of the ordinary.

I reply with a level "Okay."

"Um, did he tell you he and some teammates went out to a club in Los Angeles?"

"Yes," I reply. "It was right after their first game on the road. He said he played cards and won a little bit of cash." I laugh. "Of course, he lost it the next day."

Madison, twisting to face me more fully, questions in a serious tone, "He didn't mention anything else about that night?"

I shake my head. "No, nothing."

"Shit. What I was hoping was nothing now seems like it's something."

"Good God." I roll my eyes, losing patience. "Would you just tell me already?"

"All right." My friend, who's been holding her phone in her lap, lifts it and types in her password. Turning the device to me, she says softly, "This was posted on some kid's private Instagram. I guess he was working the door in the back room at that club and took some pictures of the guys."

When I glance down at the phone, I can't believe my eyes. But what I see is all too clear—my freaking husband is kissing some floozy chick.

But he's not really my husband.

He married me as a favor.

Easton has every right to kiss whomever he wants.

I have to remind myself of all these things, because what I feel right now is what I would be feeling if we were married for real—anger, sadness, betrayal.

I think about how I have to act upset for Madison's sake, since she thinks our marriage is genuine.

But then I realize I don't have to act.

I am hurt.

"What the fuck?" I grind out.

"Aww, Claire." Madison slides her phone onto the coffee table, shakes her head, and throws her arms around me. "I'm sorry," she says into my hair. "I am truly so, so sorry."

She thinks Easton was cheating on me, and really he wasn't. Still, I hope he didn't do anything else with that girl. With the way I feel about the kiss alone, if I were to find out he did something more with her that night, it might very well kill me.

As Madison pats me on the back, I murmur, "There has to be a logical explanation. There just must be."

Pulling back and holding my forearms, she says, "Yeah, there is. He's a big lying, cheating asshole."

"Madison!" I exclaim.

"I'm sorry." She lets go and sits back. "But it's true."

To her, it is.

Oh fuck, to the rest of the world it is too. If she found this picture, then surely others have seen it as well.

"Where did you get that image?" I ask. "You said it was on a private Instagram of someone you don't even know."

"It was," she says. "But supposedly a friend of that guy screenshotted it, as well as a bunch of other pics he took that night. That person then sent it to a hockey blog, which happens to be one I check every few days or so, because…and I'm sorry about this"—she winces—"they get the dirt. Anyway, I saw the pics and the accompanying story of where they came from this morning."

"Great," I state, my tone full of sarcasm.

My friend sighs. "If it's any solace, it's not a very well-known blog. Plus, I bet that kid lost his job for taking those photos."

Grimacing, I tell her, "Neither of those things makes me feel any better."

"I know," she says softly. And then she asks, "What are you going to do? I mean, after you kick Easton's ass and all."

That last one makes me laugh.

And I need a laugh right about now.

The idea of me kicking Easton's ass is funny.

"I don't know," I tell Madison.

But really, what *am* I going to do?

I can't expect Easton to live his life as a monk. This was bound to happen at some point.

But did he have to kiss someone in freaking public?

He should have known better.

"Do you think you'll leave him?" Madison asks quietly.

Of course I'm not going to leave him; it's not like what he did isn't "allowed" in our crazy arrangement. Not that we've ever talked about it. Though, considering what's happening now, maybe we should.

Whatever.

Shaking my head, I say to my friend, "No, I'm not going to leave him. It was just a kiss, Madison."

Her brow furrowing, she says, "That's still bad, Claire."

"It is."

She bites her lip, then asks, "And what if it was more?"

Again, I have no leg to stand on.

But she doesn't know that, so I wave my hand around dismissively and say, "I don't think he'd go that far."

She looks doubtful as she mutters, "I hope you're right."

I sigh. "Yeah, I do too."

I don't tell her this, but I plan to stay up tonight to talk to Easton about the situation we're now in. I don't care how late he comes in. I don't think I could sleep anyway. No matter how bad it may be, I need to know what happened.

Madison and I talk a little more. At one point, she checks the blog again and finds the incriminating photo is gone.

After scrolling through the other pics to double-check, she confirms, "Yeah, it's definitely been deleted."

I blow out a relieved breath, as that tells me Easton knows about the photo and has somehow addressed it.

"That's good that it's gone," I say.

"It is," Madison agrees. "But just in case he tries to deny it, I took a screenshot of the photo. Here, let me text it to you."

Oh great, now I'll have a picture of my husband kissing some other girl forever on my phone.

I'll have it forever because I have no plans to ever delete it.

No, I need it as a reminder that Easton is not really my husband.

I have to accept that and live with it, no matter how painful it has become.

Chapter

TWENTY-THREE

EASTON

I think Lennox has got this covered. He's good at putting out dumpster fires. And that fucking picture of the puck bunny kissing me is the biggest dumpster fire I've ever had to deal with up to this point in my career.

I'm usually known as the "good guy" hockey player. I maintain a clean image, and I strive to keep it that way.

But a picture of some floozy kissing me, one where it looks like I'm into it, even though I wasn't, is bad publicity.

Particularly when you're fucking married!

I knew I saw a flash.

And that damn kid with his phone out constantly.

No wonder—the jerk was secretly taking pictures of all of us.

Of course he'd get that last one in; it was too juicy not to.

That's why it went public. Though luckily for me, it was posted on a lesser-known hockey blog.

Once we found out about it this morning—and let me tell you, word travels fast among teammates—Lennox got right on it. He did so even though we had a game to prepare for against the Golden Knights, one that we, not surprisingly, lost.

There was just too much distraction.

After Lennox contacted his agent, he put the word out that the girl kissing me was all part of a friendly bet between me and him.

Oh, and that my wife knew all about it.

His agent even somehow got the blog content creator to take the shot down. I don't know how he did that, but I owe him, and I owe Lennox.

Now I just need to make sure Claire goes along with the story, and that she knows that the kiss meant nothing.

It *was* nothing, damn it.

I wasn't even kissing the girl back.

But in the picture, it's hard to tell.

I wish I could talk to Claire tonight. She didn't text or call all day, so I have a feeling she knows.

Not that I attempted to make contact either. I think this is something we need to discuss in person. I feel like I owe her an explanation face-to-face.

But unfortunately, it's now after two in the morning. I just pulled into the garage and checked the time before I shut down the engine.

The team flew back directly after the game, which is why I'm getting in so late.

Man, I'm glad there's no practice in the morning. We have the whole day off, thank fuck.

Sighing, I hop out of my Rover and head into the house.

I'll get my bags later.

It's quiet in the kitchen, the only sound my key fob dropping onto the counter. But as I walk down the hall toward the living room, I can hear that the TV is on.

Good, that means Claire is downstairs.

If she's awake, we can talk.

I venture into the living room, where I find her curled up and asleep on the sofa. She has on black yoga pants and a navy-blue tee. It looks like something she'd sleep in, so I guess she meant to go upstairs but drifted off while watching TV down here.

Speaking of which, I grab the remote from the coffee table and turn it off.

And that's when Claire stirs.

Stretching and yawning, she sits up. "Hey," she says groggily.

Thankfully, she doesn't sound mad.

"Hey," I reply. "I'm sorry I woke you up. I just got in and heard the TV."

"Yeah." She tucks a strand of hair behind her ear. "I watched your game earlier. I saw that you guys lost."

"We did." I sigh. "There was a lot going on yesterday."

Claire scoffs. "So it would appear."

Okay, she definitely knows.

I sit down on a chair by the sofa.

Normally I'd sit next to her, but with this shit going on, it just doesn't seem right.

"So, you know?" I ask. "You saw the picture?"

She blows out a breath. "I sure did."

"Claire, I can explain—"

"No," she cuts me off, putting her hand up for emphasis. "There's no need to say anything. You're free to do whatever you want, Easton."

I wince. Her words cut like a knife. I don't want to be free to kiss other women. I want to fucking kiss her.

But I can't tell her that. She clearly doesn't feel the same way. Look what she just said to me.

"Claire," I begin, because I still feel like she should know the whole truth, "I didn't kiss that girl. She caught me off guard and kissed me. She was actually trying to hook up with Lennox."

Claire chuffs, "That's a funny way to hook up with him. I mean, by kissing you, Easton."

She raises a brow, and damn, if I didn't know any better, I'd think she does care and is maybe even a little bit jealous.

Hmm, I hope so.

140

Sighing, I explain, "That chick is a puck bunny, Claire. When Lennox rejected her, she tried to hit on me."

"Oh," she says.

"By the way, the blog took that picture down."

"Yeah, I know. Was that your doing?"

"Lennox made it happen." I clarify, "Well, his agent did."

Softly, she asks, "Is there a story I should know? Like, if there are any questions that come up about this situation, what do I say?"

"There actually is a story we should go with," I say, still feeling like a jerk. "We'll say Lennox bet that girl to kiss me, and she did. It meant nothing—it was just a wager. And, for the record, it truly didn't mean anything anyway."

"Okay," she says. "I can go along with that."

I rake my fingers through my hair. "Claire, again, I'm sorry. You shouldn't have to even deal with this mess."

In a snippy tone, she replies, "Just next time make sure no one is taking a picture when some strange girl is trying to make out with you."

Okay, I deserve that.

Still, I tell her gruffly, "There won't be a next time, Claire."

She throws her hands up in the air. "How can you say that? Ugh! We really should have discussed this before we got married. But are you seriously telling me now that you don't ever plan to kiss anyone? And what about sex, Easton? Have you taken a vow of chastity?"

Anger flares. "No, Claire." I raise a damning brow. "Have you?"

Our eyes meet, and fuck, I know she cares about me and about us. She must see that I feel the same way, as she averts her gaze quickly.

I'm no better; I do the same.

What is wrong with us?

Why can't we move past this and just admit we have feelings for each other?

In my case, I guess I'm afraid. I'm in love with Claire, but I don't want to fuck up what we have.

Maybe she feels the same way.

So we're at an impasse.

"No," she says out of the blue.

Huh?

"No what?" I ask.

"No, I haven't taken a vow of chastity. But there are no prospects on the horizon at the moment. I can tell you that."

I release a breath I didn't even realize I was holding.

I also want to say, "Thank God."

But instead I go with a casual "None for me either."

"Okay." She nods. "Then I guess we'll worry about how to deal with that situation when it comes up for one of us."

Sighing, I reply, "I guess we will."

Shit, I hope it never does come up.

If she ever wants to fuck some man other than me, I don't

know what I'd do.

Maybe kill him?

An awkward silence descends, and Claire says, "I think I'm going to go up to bed now."

I sigh. "Yeah, me too."

We go to our separate rooms and separate beds, and the impasse continues.

Chapter

TWENTY-FOUR

CLAIRE

I wake up, and as I lie in bed staring up at the ceiling, the only thing I can think is that I love that stupid man. But there are days, like today, that I wish I didn't. Life would be so simple then. We could continue our not-real marriage, and no one would care if the other was caught kissing someone else.

"But I do care," I mutter.

I linger in bed all morning and then take a leisurely shower. By the time I'm bopping down the stairs in running shorts and a loose sweatshirt, it's almost one o'clock.

I expect Easton will be off doing something, but when I step into the kitchen, he's standing over by the counter making a sandwich.

Ugh, I was hoping to avoid him for a while, fearing that things might be weird today.

But when Easton hears me and turns around, he's smiling like our late-night discussion never happened.

Or that it hasn't changed a thing.

I hope that's the case.

"Someone sure slept in," he remarks teasingly.

"I know." I take a seat at the table as he resumes putting together his sandwich. "I'm just feeling kind of lazy today."

He replies, "No worries. Everyone deserves a lazy day here and there." Glancing over his shoulder, he asks. "Are you hungry? Do you want a sandwich too?"

"What kind are you having?" I ask.

"Just some turkey breast and cheese on wheat bread."

I nod. "Sounds good. I'll have one."

"You got it."

Easton finishes with the sandwiches and joins me at the table.

I'm so glad we're back to normal.

But as we're eating, and though our conversation is chill, I can't shake the feeling that something is different.

There's an underlying tense vibe in the air.

It could just be me, though. I feel more attracted to Easton than ever right now. I keep stealing glances over at him, admiring how hard his biceps and pecs look in the tight T-shirt he has on.

And the light blue color of the shirt really brings out his eyes.

He's also wearing cargo shorts, and it's all I can do to not reach over and place my hand on his thigh.

It's like my body is daring me to make a move.

I want him more today than I think I ever have. To feel his body on mine, skin to skin, and to feel him inside me.

"Ugh!" I place the sandwich I've barely touched back on the plate.

"What's wrong?" Easton asks, looking genuinely perplexed.

"Nothing." I close my eyes and wave my hand around. "I just felt a little sick there for a minute," I lie.

Come on, it's not like I can tell him I'm lusting for him like never before.

What if he wants to act on it?

I would.

Oh, I would.

I have no more control or will to say no.

But I must be strong.

Our whole friendship could be ruined.

Damn it, though, I want more.

I want Easton in *all* ways.

I want him to be in love with me like I am with him. And I want to make love, not fuck. Well, okay, I want that too. But not *just* that.

Frustrated, I say, "You know what? I think I need some fresh air."

I push my chair back and stand, and Easton asks, "Do you want me to come with you?"

Normally, I would say, "Sure," but right now, I need to be alone.

Shaking my head, I tell him, "No, that's okay. Finish your sandwich."

With the look he's giving me, it's clear he knows something is wrong.

It is wrong.

Everything is wrong.

And I have no idea how to ever make it right again.

Chapter

TWENTY-FIVE

EASTON

Damn. Is Claire still mad about that picture? I really thought we had it all worked out after our talk last night.

But if we're okay, why did she just leave half her sandwich on the plate and run outside?

Stranger still, she didn't want me to come with her.

That's not like her.

That's not like *us*.

What I'd like to do is go outside and take her in my arms. I'd tell her that somewhere along the line, I've fallen in love with her.

Or I don't know, maybe I always have been?

But I can't go to her right now. I can't tell her anything. She's clearly still pissed at me.

Hell, knowing Claire, she'd probably punch me.

But even worse, what if I came clean and she told me she doesn't love me? At least not in the same way.

That would fucking crush my heart.

We'd have to get a divorce. Something we never bring up but will probably happen.

But I don't want a divorce.

I want to stay married to Claire.

I just wish we could be a true husband and wife.

Someday we're going to have to address this.

But not today.

No, today I'll just finish my sandwich and give her some space.

A week goes by, and things with Claire and I remain the same—tense and weird. It doesn't help that one of the days I have that lunch with the girl who won at the charity auction.

Claire knows and acts like she doesn't care. But there's clear relief on her face when I return and tell her a team representative joined us. It wasn't just me and the girl.

And so life goes on…

The rest of the week, there are moments when it feels like we're back to normal. Like the other day when we took a hike, everything was fabulous. We laughed and talked and even hung out at the table by Stan for a while.

But then, once we returned to the house, that strange awkwardness came roaring back.

Same thing the other night.

I asked Claire if she wanted to watch a movie. She was all into it and even more excited when I suggested a romantic comedy, a true chick flick.

Hey, I'm willing to do anything to make her happy at this point.

Anyway, once the movie started, I thought we were having a good time. We were joking around and commenting on the funny parts.

But then a love scene came on, and Claire abruptly got up and left.

I didn't even get an explanation.

I thought at first that she had just run to the bathroom.

But she never returned.

When I asked her the next day what happened, she just shrugged it off and said she got really tired and went to bed.

Yeah, right.

When she realized I wasn't buying it at all, she tried to tell me that she didn't really like the movie.

I just kept thinking how she was into it up to that point. I guess that love scene really turned her off.

Hmm, wonder why?

I didn't call her out, though.

I just said, "You should have told me you didn't like it. We could have put on something else."

"Nah, it's okay," she replied. "I truly was exhausted too. I didn't even have the energy to come back down and tell you I was done for the night."

Ahh, we were back to that bullshit.

Hell, it wasn't even that late when she bailed on me.

But, again, I kept all that to myself.

Today I'm golfing with Lennox and Shane. I don't even know what Claire is up to. She was already gone from the house when I got up.

"Easton, you're up," Lennox says, jarring me from my thoughts.

I was totally zoning out.

"I'm on it," I reply as I walk over to the green and tee up the ball.

I think about all my frustration with Claire, and when I take a swing, I knock that motherfucker almost all the way to the next green.

"Holy shit," Shane says. "Nice shot, man."

"Thanks," I murmur.

We're on the fourth hole, and I've been kicking ass so far. When you're dealing with a lot of confusion, whacking the shit out of something is very cathartic.

But I guess I'm not hiding my feelings all that well, seeing as, while Shane tees up, Lennox asks me, "Is everything okay at home?"

I play dumb. "You mean with Claire?"

"Uh-huh."

"Yeah, sure," I reply with way too much enthusiasm. "Things are great."

Okay, that was over the top, and Lennox knows it.

We're silent as we watch Shane hit the ball off to the tree line on the right.

I'm safe from further interrogation, because we have to pile into the golf cart and drive down to where Shane's ball is in the rough.

Then again, maybe I'm not so safe, seeing as Lennox starts it back up when he asks, "Claire's not still mad about that picture, is she?"

Shane, who's driving the cart, jumps in. "You still in trouble, man? You know, we can talk to her if you want."

"No, no," I reply. "I appreciate the offer, guys. I really do. But like I said, everything is super. She's not mad about anything."

"That's good," Shane says.

They seem to accept my explanation.

We reach the tree line, and thankfully the subject is changed back to golf.

But Claire is still on my mind.

Part of what I told them is true—she's not mad about the

picture. At least I don't think she is.

But there is a problem of some sort, and I fear it's far deeper.

The scariest part is, I have a feeling whatever this tension is between me and Claire, it's about to blow way the fuck up.

I just hope we both survive.

Chapter

TWENTY-SIX

CLAIRE

Yesterday, when Easton went to play golf with the guys, he didn't know it, but I was meeting with my attorneys. I wanted to see if my dad could revoke my trust fund if we were to ever get divorced.

The answer is that he can't.

The money is mine.

When Easton returned home, I wanted to tell him what I'd found out. This way he'll know he's not trapped and stuck with me forever. He can have a life with a real wife and everything that goes with that.

Problem was, I couldn't build up enough courage to bring up

the subject. The truth is, I don't want a divorce. I'd like to stay married to Easton. I don't want him to be free to find someone else. *I* want to have a real marriage with him.

I just don't know how he'd feel about that.

And that's what scares me.

So, when he walked into the house yesterday, I just asked him about his golf game.

He said he'd won.

We were in the kitchen, and we just kind of stood there then, at a loss for words.

That's been happening a lot lately.

Huffing, I started to walk away.

But then he stopped me when he said, "Can you hold up a sec? I forgot to tell you something."

I turned back to face him, hoping he'd say he's fallen in love with me, and can we stop this farce of a fake marriage.

But no, he just said, "I have practice tomorrow morning, and that pool repair guy I told you about is coming at ten. I should be back around eleven, but can you let him in and stick around till I'm home? You know, in case he needs something."

"Repair guy?" I questioned, 'cause I had no idea one was even coming. "Is there something wrong with the pool?"

"Yeah," Easton replied. "I guess I forgot to tell you. The pump in the infinity pool isn't working right. We need to have it looked at. I called the shop the other day and made the appointment. I'm sorry. I really thought I had mentioned it."

"I guess we've had a lot on our minds lately," I said, waiting for his reaction.

He glanced at me, but then he looked away. "Yeah, I guess so."

Ugh, I hate this.

"It's okay," I assured him, getting back to the pool issue. "I'll be here. I'll let the guy in and stick around till you're home."

"Great."

He showed me a picture of the repair man and told me the company informs you via text so you don't let in the wrong person. I think that's a good idea, seeing as you can never be too careful nowadays.

I didn't say anything when I saw the photo, but I was immediately struck by how freaking hot the guy is. He's young and has blond hair and surfer-dude good looks.

I was sure to play it cool and nonchalant, but in my head, I was coming up with a plan, a plan I'm about to implement today. Because today is pool repair day, and Easton is at practice.

Yeah, it's time to make a bold move to see just how much my fake husband cares about me. And I mean in a romantic way. I'm tired of wondering and guessing. This could go on forever if someone doesn't do something.

So, I'm on it.

I check the time and discover it's almost ten.

Great.

I'm pretty much ready to go downstairs and put my plan into motion. But before I do, I take one final look in the full-length mirror in my bedroom.

My chestnut locks are tumbling down my back in soft curls, and I have my cutest sunglasses perched up on my head. I put on some liner and mascara earlier to enhance my eyes, but the coup de grâce is what I'm wearing.

Or rather how little I have on.

Yep, I'm in a skimpy siren-red bikini. My breasts are practically spilling over the top, and the bottoms leave little to the imagination, as they expose quite a bit of my ass cheeks.

Ahhh, I have to chuckle.

This poor pool guy is not going to know what hit him.

And neither will Easton when he gets home.

This is going to be epic.

Hey, desperate times call for desperate measures, right?

One of us needs to make a bold move to elicit a reaction. If Easton comes home and doesn't care that I'm outside flirting with the pool guy in a barely there bikini, then I'll finally know for sure that he truly only sees me as a friend.

But if he gets jealous, well, then all bets are off. Maybe we can finally move forward and end this farce.

I smile at the thought, but then I'm startled as the doorbell rings.

Oh my God!

Hot pool guy is here.

"Showtime," I murmur as I run out of my room and race down the stairs.

When I pop open the front door, there stands Mr. Hot Surfer Dude.

My, he is fine.

He's even better-looking in person.

Easton is going to be so mad.

That is, he will be if he cares.

I welcome the pool guy in and, checking out his name tag, I say, "You can follow me out back, Brant. I'll show you where the pool is. I was on my way out there anyway."

It takes a beat for him to react, as he's too busy checking me out.

Perfect.

This is going just as planned.

"Oh, okay," he says at last. "Thank you."

I can't help but smile as he follows me through the house. I know he is totally staring at my ass.

Once we're out back, I gesture to the infinity pool and let him know I'll be hanging on a chaise lounge nearby catching some rays.

"If you need anything, like a bottle of water or a Coke or something, just let me know," I say cheerily as I plop down on a padded lounger and lower my sunglasses to my face. "Oh, and by the way, my name is Claire."

Might as well be on a first-name basis here, right?

Swallowing hard as he tries not to stare at my chest, he says, "Okay, sounds good. I'll let you know if I get thirsty, Claire."

Damn, you look like you already are.

Of course, I don't say that. I just go with a slightly suggestive "You do that."

Brant walks away to work on the pool, and I lean back, smiling.

I can't wait for Easton to get home and find me out here.

This is so on.

Chapter

TWENTY-SEVEN

EASTON

Practice ends, and I shower and dress in dark cargo shorts, a beige tee, and flip-flops so quickly it's not even funny. I then bust my ass to get home.

Hey, I noticed how good-looking that fucking pool repair guy is. I don't want him alone with Claire for too long.

Hopefully, she'll just let him in, take him out to the pool, and then head back inside.

That's what I'd do.

But once I'm home, I can't find Claire anywhere inside the house.

Fuck.

Blowing out one long, deep breath, I head to the back and step outside.

That's when I freeze.

The repair guy is standing over by the pool, and there's Claire, right next to him. She's signing something on a clipboard, before she hands it back to the guy.

What really gets me, though, is throughout this whole exchange, the two of them are laughing and chatting it up like they're old friends.

But the absolute worst part is what Claire has on—practically nothing!

Her breasts are squeezed up and overflowing the too-small red bikini top, and the bottom part is little more than a thong.

I catch the pool dude checking her out, and she doesn't even seem to care. If I didn't know any better, I'd think she's encouraging it.

And enjoying the attention.

But why would she do that?

Why would she like being ogled?

They're so busy talking that neither of them even notices me. But when Claire touches the dude's forearm, giggling over something he just said, I make my presence known.

Marching over to where they're standing, I bark out, "What the fuck is going on here?"

The pool repair guy looks terrified, but Claire just stares me down angrily, her hazel eyes narrowing, those flecks of gold and green sparking with rage.

Huffing, she informs me curtly, "I was signing off on the completed work and billing, Easton. That's what's going on."

"And you're doing that dressed in an outfit like this?" I wave my hand up and down her body.

The repair guy, looking nervous, jumps in. "Sir, uh, the pump is fixed. It didn't take as long as I expected. Anyway, I think I'll be leaving now."

"Good idea," I growl. With my eyes locked with Claire's, I add a more even, "Thank you."

Claire, smiling smugly at me and never wavering in glaring back, says in an oh-so-sweet tone, "Yes, thank you, Brant. It was nice talking with you."

He mumbles, "Bye, Claire," and then he takes off so quickly he's like a blur.

Now that he's gone, it's just me and Claire, still engaged in a stare-down.

"Brant?" I say, raising a brow. "And he knows your name too? You two sure got chummy in a short amount of time."

"What can I say?" She shrugs. "We hit it off really well right from the start."

"Clearly," I grind out, my temper flaring.

"He's so cute too," she goes on in a sing-song tone. "Did you notice that?"

Okay, she's looking for a reaction now, so I rasp, "Fuck him."

I'm angry, yes, but Claire shows me she might be madder than me when she jabs a finger in my chest and says, "By the way, for the record, don't you ever embarrass me like that again, Easton."

With that, she spins around and struts away, tossing the sunglasses that were perched on her head onto a nearby table.

"Ah, not so fast there, sweetheart," I spit out as I kick off my flip-flops and follow her.

The whole while, as mad as I am, my eyes stay fixed on her glorious, perky ass. An ass that fucking dickhead got to enjoy the entire time I was gone. I wonder if the pump really is fixed after all.

We reach the house, and Claire races inside.

I grab the sliding door before she can shut it, and she blurts out, "Asshole," as she marches away.

"Asshole?" I laugh bitterly as I follow her.

We reach the entry hall, and she steps over to the base of the staircase.

"And what's this about me embarrassing you?" I state gruffly. "You running around flirting with that dude dressed in next to nothing is fucking embarrassing to *me*, honey."

She spins around, her hand slamming down on the handrail post. "Oh, really?" she says. "Let me make this clear, Easton. What I do, including flirting with other guys, and what I wear to do it in is of no concern to you."

"Well, maybe it should be," I spit out.

That catches her off guard, as she has nothing to say, no smart retort, not a thing.

I take a step closer till she moves to one step above me.

We're now face-to-face, both of us worked up and breathing hard.

Her eyes meet mine, and the anger within them in is palpable.

But there's also lust and confusion.

That calms me down.

She bites her lip, and I blow out a breath. "Look, Claire—"

Placing one finger over my mouth, like she's shushing me, she says, "Easton, just shut up. For once, stop."

I do.

Slowly, she trails her finger over my lips.

What is happening here?

I'm confused as she leans in and presses her mouth to mine, kissing me softly at first, then more demandingly.

Okay, now I'm not confused.

I open my mouth, and our tongues intertwine.

And it is fucking divine.

Finally, I'm kissing Claire the way I've wanted to for ages.

As we relax, she presses her breasts against me.

All I want to do is rip this damn T-shirt up and over my head.

Hey, I think I will.

I break from kissing Claire just long enough to ditch the tee.

And then my lips are back on hers.

She pushes into me again, and I realize she's untied the bikini top and let it drop to the step she's on.

Suddenly, her bare skin and pert nipples are rubbing against my bare chest.

Fuck.

That's it.

I reach down to grab her supple ass and give her cheeks a squeeze, something I've wanted to do since she stomped away from the pool.

I then step back, pick Claire up, and carry her up to my bedroom.

This is our time, at last, and nothing is going to stop what's about to happen.

Only she can.

Chapter

TWENTY-EIGHT

CLAIRE

"**T**ell me to put you down," Easton says gruffly as he carries me up the stairs. "Here's your chance, Claire."

Is he kidding?

I've been waiting for this forever.

So I say nothing. I just hold onto him, my free hand rubbing his smooth, bare chest, and then reaching up to touch his face.

It's like I can't get enough of him.

I've wanted to touch him like this for so damn long.

Outside his bedroom, he stops and looks down at me. "Are you sure you want to do this? One last chance. 'Cause when we go in there, we're not coming out for a good long while."

"I wouldn't want it any other way," I reply.

"Good," he says as he kicks open the door with his bare foot.

And then I'm on the bed, Easton hovering over me. "Hey, I love you," he tells me.

I'm floored. "What?"

I wasn't expecting him to say that, though it does fill my heart with joy.

But does he love me?

Like, *really* love me?

With his hand on my cheek, caressing ever so softly, he says, "Yes, I love you, Claire." He goes on, pouring out his heart. "I don't mean just as a friend, though I love you in that way too. I always have, since we were kids. But I'm *in* love with you as well."

"Easton." Tears well in my eyes, and as they start to fall, he wipes them away. "I love you too," I tell him. "In all the same ways. I'm in love with you so much that there are days when keeping it to myself actually hurts."

Chuckling, he says, "We've been fools, haven't we? Feeling the same way about each other but afraid to say it out loud."

"I didn't want to lose you as my friend," I confess, my tears subsiding. "Having at least part of your heart was better than having nothing at all."

"Claire…" His eyes hold mine. "You have *all* of my heart. And you always will."

"You have mine too," I share.

And then I let out a small laugh.

"What?" he asks.

"I guess little Lydia was right all along."

"She was," he agrees, leaning down to kiss me.

As our kiss intensifies, our tongues entwining and our breathing picking up, I murmur between kisses, "God, I want you."

Pulling back slightly, he says, "Fuck. I want you, too, Claire. I have for what feels like forever."

"Seriously." I laugh. "I know the feeling."

I'm so anxious and excited, but we still have some clothes on.

Ugh.

Time to remedy that.

Sitting up, Easton takes off his shorts and boxer briefs while I wiggle out of my bikini bottoms.

Naked and bare and oh so beautiful, Easton leans over to open a drawer in the nightstand by the bed, where he pulls out a strip of condoms.

When he sets them on top of the nightstand, within easy reach, I remark, "Wow. Are those all for tonight?"

Grinning, he says, "Yeah. We have a lot of time to make up for, you know?"

"Isn't that the truth? So…" I pull him down to me, my lips grazing his. "Let's get started."

Chapter

TWENTY-NINE

EASTON

I do everything to and with Claire that I've longed to do for over a decade, using my hands, my mouth, and my cock. And though I have her slowly and sweetly the first time, our second round is hot, sweaty, and just plain wild. It's like everything we've been holding back for so long finally gets released.

"Damn," I breathe as I fall back onto the pillows.

"Right?" Claire turns to her side and starts tracing small circles on my bare chest as she murmurs, "This should have been our wedding night."

I raise a brow. "In Vegas?"

She nods once. "Uh-huh."

"Nah." I shake my head. "I'm glad we're in my bed. We can stay here forever, and we never have to check out."

That makes her laugh. "Forever? Uh, I think we'll have to leave sometime."

"Yeah, but—" I roll over onto her. "—not for a while."

Time number three goes down in the books.

And then we're on to the shower.

Shower sex with Claire has been a huge fantasy of mine. I guess because I've spent so much time in there jerking off while thinking about her.

Let me tell you, the real thing is so much better.

We christen her room too.

Oh, and the living room.

Even the kitchen is not off-limits.

By the time the sun starts to rise, that strip of condoms is indeed gone. And I am fucking exhausted. As is Claire.

I don't have practice this morning, and she has nothing planned either, so, wrapped in each other's arms, we finally get some much-needed sleep.

It is the best rest I've ever had.

Chapter

THIRTY

CLAIRE

'm on cloud nine. No, really—I feel so happy it's like I'm really walking on air. In fact, I'm practically skipping when I head into the upscale downtown restaurant where I'm meeting Madison for lunch.

She's waiting just inside the lobby, and when she sees me, she says, "My, don't you look pretty today." I have on a lavender sheath dress and cream-colored heels.

"Thanks," I reply, then, gesturing to her, I say, "You're looking quite stunning as well."

Madison is always so put together, and today is no exception. She's wearing a black pencil skirt with matching Louboutin pumps and a red silk blouse. Her gorgeous blonde locks are in a perfect

French braid trailing down her back.

After we're seated at a table along a painting-lined wall, and the host hands us each a menu, I catch Madison staring at me thoughtfully.

"What?" I ask.

"It's nothing bad," she assures me. "It's just that what I said in the lobby is true. You look really, really great today. But it's more than your outfit. You have a glow." She pauses, then just flat-out states, "You look like you had some exceptionally good sex with your husband this morning."

"As a matter of fact," I say, grinning, "we totally did."

It feels so good to finally have a "real" husband and not have to deflect these types of inquiries.

"Okay, okay," she says, waving her cloth napkin around before placing it on her lap. "I don't need any details, though. I've been in a drought lately. I swear all the good ones are taken. You're so lucky, Claire."

After she found out the cheating thing was all a big misunderstanding, Madison was back on Team Easton. But she's right—I really am lucky. And again, it feels good to have a real marriage with Easton with all the marital benefits, like the amazing sex we really did have this morning.

Oh, and also last night.

And—

"Claire," Madison says, breaking me from my sex-reverie. "Do you know what you want, or do you need more time?"

When I look up from my menu, I realize the server is waiting for me. She must've just asked me the exact same question.

"Oh, crap." I quickly peruse the selections, but I'm undecided. "I'm sorry," I say. "Can I have another minute or so, please?"

The young lady smiles and tells me, "Of course. Take your time. I'll be back over in a few."

"Thank you."

As I look over the menu, I ask Madison, "What are you having?"

She says, "The grilled chicken with mixed greens."

"Oooh, that sounds tasty. I think I'll get the same thing."

This time when the server returns, I'm ready. We place our orders, and she walks away.

I then ask Madison, "What do you have planned after lunch?"

After taking a quick sip of ice water, she replies, "I'm showing a nice townhouse over in Scottsdale at two. What about you?"

"I have a check I need to drop off at the children's hospital. Some of our new corporate sponsors made donations, and I'm matching them."

"That's great." Madison smiles at me. "I love that your foundation has really taken off. It's for such a good cause too."

"Thanks, and it really is. Oh, and I forgot to tell you that Easton and I are thinking of starting another charity. This time we're considering something to help animals in need of care and homes."

"Aww," Madison coos. "I love the idea of that one too."

We talk some more, and when our lunches arrive, we devour them. The grilled chicken is beyond divine. I'm glad I chose it.

Since we have places we need to be, we pay the bill, wrap up with a big hug and a promise to talk soon, and then we go our separate ways.

After my meeting with some of the hospital big shots, who are thrilled with the monetary donations, I decide to go upstairs to check in on Lydia. I kind of want to let her know she was right all along.

I'm hoping it may give her a little joy to hear that and to know I remembered what she said.

But just as I'm about to step into her hospital room, a stern-looking nurse stops me. "Excuse me, ma'am, but you can't go in there."

"Oh," I say, stepping back. I explain, "I know the patient that's in there. I was just going to stop by and say hi."

The nurse pshaws. "How do you know the patient? The child in there is only three."

Confused, I say, "Wait." I look at the room number again to make sure I'm at the correct spot. When I verify that I am, I ask,

"Isn't this Lydia's room?"

The nurse's expression softens. "Oh, I'm sorry. Hasn't anyone told you?"

I feel sick. "Told me what?" I ask.

Placing her hand on my forearm, she says delicately, "Miss Lydia passed away a week ago."

"Wait, what?" Tears well in my eyes as I choke out, "No, that can't be true. Please tell me it's not."

Squeezing my arm gently, the nurse says, "I'm sorry. But it's true."

I know I'm about to break down, so I just apologize and take off. I want to get home to Easton. He needs to know this awful news as well.

I make it to my car, somehow holding it together.

But once the door is closed, I place my head in my hands and just completely lose it.

THIRTY-ONE

EASTON

When I return from my late-morning practice, I notice Claire's car is parked in front of the house and not in the garage. It's also kind of askew, like she was in a rush or something.

This is odd.

And that makes me worry right away.

I hope everything is okay. I mean, she had a lunch with Madison planned, then a stop at the children's hospital to drop off a check.

Concerned, I pull up behind her and cut the engine.

I'm out the door of my Rover and in the house in no time.

"Claire?" I call out.

There's a soft whimpering coming from the living room, and then I hear a choked-up "I'm in here."

Jesus, what could be going on?

I swear, if someone hurt my wife, there will be hell to pay.

In the living room, Claire is curled up in a corner of the sofa. She has on a pretty lavender dress, and her heels are lying on the floor. And though she's always beautiful to me, her face is red, and tears are streaming down her cheeks.

"Oh my God." I race over and sit down next to her, picking up her hand. "What's going on? Did something happen?"

Clearly, something occurred to upset her, so that was a stupid thing to say.

Claire nods. "It's Lydia," she chokes out.

"Lydia?" It takes me a beat, but then I realize who she means. And she was just at the children's hospital. "Oh, Lydia. Is she okay?"

"No," Claire sobs. "She's dead, Easton."

I freeze. "Holy shit! What?"

Recognizing how tragic this is, I throw my arms around Claire. We hold onto each other for comfort. I'm not a big crier, but I can feel my eyes watering at the loss of that special little girl.

How can this be?

Obviously, Lydia was very sick, but I guess we always assumed she was improving. I mean, she was so vibrant and so in-the-moment with life.

And she knew things.

She sure called it with us.

Claire, composing herself somewhat, pulls back. She swipes tears away from her cheeks while I discreetly rub my eyes.

Softly, I ask, "What happened?"

Blowing out a breath, she says, "After I dropped off the check at the hospital, I decided to go upstairs to visit Lydia. I wanted to tell her how right she was about us." She stops and smiles sadly at me, and I give her a small smile back. "Anyway, when I reached her room, a nurse stopped me from going in. She said there was someone else in there. I just figured Lydia had been moved. But then…" She sighs, and I take her hand again. "The nurse gave me the sad news."

"I can't believe it." I murmur, shaking my head.

Claire squeezes my hand. "I know. She was truly someone special."

An idea pops into my head, and I say, "You know what? We should do something to honor her memory."

Claire nods. "Like having a plaque installed at the hospital, or maybe dedicating a bench to her? They could place it out in their atrium with all the flower gardens."

"We can do those things," I reply. "But I was thinking of something more personal. Something involving us that she would approve of and be proud of the two of us for finally admitting our true feelings for each other."

Looking intrigued, Claire asks, "What did you have in mind?"

Now it's my turn to squeeze her hand as I say, "Let's get married."

She laughs. "We already are, you silly man."

"No, I know. But I mean let's have the wedding we should have had. Our Vegas ceremony will always hold a special place in my heart, but I love you so much, Claire. I want all of our family and friends to be there to witness our vows. Well," I clarify, "technically, it'd be a vow renewal. But that's okay, right?"

Claire is smiling, and there's happiness in her eyes.

I'm glad I was able to find a way to make her feel better.

"Yes," she says, nodding. "I love that idea. And Easton?"

"Yes?"

"I love you so damn much."

"Babe, I love you too."

Chapter

THIRTY-TWO

CLAIRE

Easton's idea for us to have a big wedding with all of our family and friends to honor Lydia is a great idea. But it's more than that—it's for us too. We need to celebrate what we've finally realized we have with each other—true, everlasting love.

That's why, when we begin to plan our celebration, it's important to us to make sure everything is perfect.

We start by doing the things we didn't do the first time around.

For one, Easton officially asks my mom, and even my dad, for my hand in marriage. He explains to them that though it will technically be a vow renewal, we're treating it like a full-on first wedding.

Mom is ecstatic, and my father...well, he's my typical stoic dad.

But of course they give their blessings.

Second order of business is that I take Madison out to lunch so I can ask her to be my maid of honor, something she's wanted since we became friends.

When I finally toss it out there, casually before the food arrives at our table, she's so excited that she squeals and hops out of her chair. She runs over to my side, bends down, and throws her arms around me.

"Wow," I say, laughing as I hug her back. "I guess that's a yes?"

"Yes, yes, yes," she replies before letting me go and straightening up. "Absolutely." Peering down at me, she asks coyly, "By the way, is Lennox going to be Easton's best man?"

I laugh. "As a matter of fact, he is. We're only having you two as attendants. We want to keep the bridal party small since everything else is turning out to be so big."

"Understandable," she says, nodding.

I watch her closely as I ask, "Is there something going on with you and Lennox?"

"No." She shakes her head, acting all innocent as she trots back to her side of the table and plops down in her seat. "I just still think he's hot as hell."

Hmmm, I'm not sure if I believe her. She looks like she's keeping a secret. But digging deeper into this is a task for another day.

Because I have a wedding to plan!

And plan I do.

Easton and I choose a nice church and rent out a beautiful reception space. With Madison's help, I find the prettiest silk and lace wedding gown to wear. She opts for a long maid of honor dress.

Also, the guys pick out and rent their tuxedos.

And then there's everything else that Easton and I slowly check off—invitations, the music, flowers, the cake...

The list goes on and on.

In the end, the only things we don't need are rings. We have our simple platinum bands that we picked out in Vegas.

I look down at my left hand now and smile as I think about that day and how far we've come.

I'm waiting for Easton in the entry hall of our house, dressed in a shimmery silver dress with spaghetti straps and a pair of high heels. The dressy look is for a reason—Easton is taking me out to dinner tonight to a fancy restaurant. He said that he wants to celebrate that the wedding is now only a week away and we, at last, have everything finalized.

He had a quick errand to run before we leave for the restaurant. That's why I'm waiting.

A few minutes pass, and then I hear his Range Rover pulling up outside.

I'd normally just go out, but he insisted before he left that he wants to come to the door and pick me up like a "real" date.

He's such a romantic.

After we complete that formality, we head out to the vehicle with Easton holding my hand.

When we reach the passenger door, he opens it for me.

I say, "Thanks," then add, "You look really handsome tonight, by the way."

He replies, "Not as good as you, babe. But thank you anyway."

We reach the restaurant, and the booth we're given has a giant window, affording us beautiful views of the mountains in the distance and the setting sun.

"This is so nice," I say to Easton.

"Only the best for my beautiful wife."

"Aww," I coo. "You're so sweet. You know what? You're so wonderful, I think I'll marry you again."

"Speaking of which," he says as he slips out of the booth and walks over to my side. "I wanted to wait until after dinner, but I can't."

No sooner do I get the words "Wait for what?" out of my mouth, Easton is dropping down to one knee and holding out the most stunning diamond engagement ring I think I've ever seen.

"I never gave you a proper proposal with a ring, Claire, so I want to do so now." He clears his throat and goes on. "Claire Weller, will you marry me again and accept this ring as a token of all of our love?"

'Yes, yes," I say excitedly.

This is actually our third proposal. I once asked him all those years ago when we were seventeen, and he asked me when we reunited out here in Arizona.

But this proposal is by far the best.

Easton slips the ring onto my finger and stands up.

But before he heads back over to his side of the booth, he leans down, and we share a kiss.

When he turns around, to our surprise, the people in the restaurant and the staff break out in raucous applause.

Wow, I didn't even realize anyone was paying attention.

But I'm glad they were and are, in a way, celebrating with us.

And it is a celebration. Even our waiter presents us with a complimentary bottle of champagne.

We go on to have a wonderful dinner while the sun sizzles down behind the mountains. Once it's dark out, the sky fills with a million twinkling stars.

It's the perfect ending to a perfect night with the most perfect man and the promise of a perfect life.

EPILOGUE

EASTON

We have our dream wedding, and it is everything we hoped it would be and more.

The hockey season continues, and there are games we win and games we lose. But the losses don't sting quite as much as they once did. Not when the most important thing in my life now is my beautiful wife and our life together.

Truly, I can't imagine things getting any better.

I feel like I'm at the top.

But then one day in March, Claire tells me she's pregnant. We weren't actively trying, but we weren't doing anything to prevent it either. We figured if it happens, it happens.

I was hoping it would, and I think Claire was too.

And now it has.

Fuck, I am so excited!

I thought I'd reached the top, but now I'm at an even higher level of happiness.

How could life get any better now?

But it does—the day our daughter is born.

I discover a whole new level of joy, one I never dreamed possible.

Man, that little girl is perfection.

And so is our son when he's born two years later.

And our second daughter, whom we name Lydia, born just last week.

I think back to all those years ago and the walk I was taking with Claire when she asked me if I'd marry her when she turned twenty-seven. That is, if we were both still single.

I said "yes," of course.

And you know what? It was never about helping her get her trust fund. I know now that I loved her way back then.

She's since told me that she's always loved me too.

It just took us ten years to figure it out.

Ha!

But the important thing is that we did.

Yeah, from two little kids meeting in the neighborhood, to

becoming best friends in our teenage years, to falling in love back then but being too scared to recognize it, to moving away and drifting apart, to reuniting and getting married as a fulfillment of a promise, to falling in love all over again and marrying once more, this time for love, to having our kids and creating a beautiful life.

From where we've been to where we are.

Some things in life are meant to be, and nothing can stop it.

And that is the story of me and Claire.

The End

Up next in this new *Glacier Hockey* romance series of interconnected standalones is book #2—*Lennox*— releasing October 2025!

ABOUT THE AUTHOR

S.R. Grey is a USA Today Bestselling Author of the new Glacier Hockey series, the bestselling Breakaway hockey series and Boys of Winter hockey books, and the Men of Fall football novels. Other New Adult and Romantic Suspense works of hers include the Judge Me Not books, the Promises series, the Inevitability duology, A Harbour Falls Mystery trilogy, and the Laid Bare series of novellas.

Ms. Grey resides in Pennsylvania. When not writing, she can be found reading, traveling, running, or cheering for her hometown sports teams, sometimes all at the same time.

S.R. Grey's Author Website:

http://srgrey.com/

S.R. Grey on Facebook:

http://www.facebook.com/SRGrey

S.R. Grey's FB Reading Group:

https://www.facebook.com/groups/

SRGreyHardAbsandHotBooks/

S.R. Grey on BookBub:

https://www.bookbub.com/authors/s-r-grey

S.R. Grey on X/Twitter:

https://twitter.com/AuthorSRGrey

S.R. Grey on Instagram:

https://www.instagram.com/authorsrgrey/

S.R. Grey Goodreads Author page:

http://www.goodreads.com/author/show/6433082.S_R_Grey

Wait!

It's not over yet.

Check out the first chapter of **Destiny on Ice**, the beginning of my bestselling *Boys of Winter* hockey rom-com series.

ONE

GOLDEN BOY GETS A LITTLE TARNISHED

BRENT

My father was a great hockey player. Back in the day, in the era of eighties' big hair and synthesized music, Billy Oliver won not just one, but two Stanley Cups. He was awarded the Conn Smythe trophy both times and has received an assortment of other hardware throughout the years.

He's retired now, but my dad was once a star.

To me, though, he's always just been Dad.

But as his only child, I have a legacy to live up to. I pray I don't disappoint him. I pray someday I'll be as good as he once was. And damn it, I better win a freaking Stanley Cup like he did.

I have no choice, not really. Since the moment my father first laced up hockey skates on my three-year-old little feet, the look of pride on his face told me even then all I needed to know— anything short of being the best will never do.

And guess what?

In many ways, I've become the best at what I do, which is, like my dad, play professional hockey.

I've been good since the start, a natural some say. I don't know about that, but I do know that even before I was drafted—in the first round by the Las Vegas Wolves, an expansion team at the time—I was being called "The Golden Boy" and "The Next One."

These days, three years later, I'm pretty much the poster boy for the NHL. And I have a slew of endorsement deals to prove it.

Lately, though, I've been falling short.

And I really don't know why.

Something is missing for me in the game. Or is it something that's missing in *me*?

I blow out a breath and shake my head.

Things started out so great. Where'd it all go wrong?

I made a name for myself early on. Expansion teams usually struggle for years before posting a winning record. Not so for the Wolves. With me centering what was then a subpar line, I was still able to make us shine. We came out swinging that first season in the league.

BRENT OLIVER SCORES THE GAME-WINNING GOAL IN HIS AND THE WOLVES' FIRST NHL GAME, SETS UP TEAMMATES FOR TWO MORE

One month later, there was this:

THE WOLVES OFF TO A COMPLETELY UNEXPECTED STELLAR START

Then things started to slide.

Those subpar players on my line weren't enough to keep afloat a pretty much overall crappy team, even with me centering. The Wolves' owners and management made the necessary moves—they don't mess around when shit needs to get done.

We picked up a phenomenal winger, Nolan Solvenson. He started to play and things turned around.

ADDING SKILLED RIGHT-WINGER NOLAN SOLVENSON TO ROOKIE BRENT OLIVER'S FIRST LINE PROVING TO BE A MASTERFUL MOVE

ON A MID-SEASON WINNING STREAK, THAT SOLVENSON TRADE IS PAYING OFF FOR THE WOLVES!

Another trade made at the deadline gave us Benjamin Perry. A big, strong left-handed winger, he was the final piece to the puzzle. Even with far-from-elite second, third, and fourth lines, it didn't matter. Not with me, Benjamin, and Nolan on the first line. We could *not* be stopped.

Benjamin—or Benny, as he's known to the team—is adept at using his size and muscle to check the hell out of any sorry soul who happens to be matched up against him. He simply wears other players down…and then it's a fucking scorefest. Thanks, in part, to his killer slapshot.

Together with Nolan, a sniper in his own right, we were—and in many ways still are—quite a force to be reckoned with. We destroy teams, though not as much lately. But back then, man, we were racking up so many points that the press branded us the OPS line, as in Special Forces.

THE OPS LINE'S SNIPERS OF OLIVER, PERRY, AND SOLVENSON ELIMINATE THE COMPETITION WITH EASE
THERE'S NOTHING COVERT ABOUT THIS LINE'S SCORING PROWESS

We worked our reputation to our advantage. Trash-talking on the ice and taunting players became our pastimes. We also happened to get a lot of pucks in the net.

Ah, the good old days.

We still trash-talk and taunt, but we aren't as lethal as we once were.

"We just need to get back on track," I murmur to myself. "The season doesn't start for a few more weeks. I'll have my shit together by then."

I better, since I'm the captain of the team. If I go down, we all sink. And that's not fair to anyone, especially not to my linemates, Nolan and Benny. Over the past couple of years they've become my best friends, which is a blessing and a curse. It's a blessing that we play so well together, but it's a curse that we also have a tendency to fuel each other's vices.

God knows this off-season we've become far too focused on partying and women. Like me, my linemates are extremely popular. Hell, let's not mince words—we're gods. In the hockey world, it's good to be a god. Guys want to *be* you and girls want to *do* you. Multiply that all by a hundred if you're not an ogre in the looks department.

And none of us are.

Not to brag—though, I guess I kind of am—but I have the most women falling at my feet. Hell, I've had women who've wanted to *lick* my feet.

Like, literally.

There was this crazy bitch this one time…

Wait, I digress. Back to where our team is today—floundering in a sea of mediocrity.

After that first good regular season, we fell apart during the playoffs. A dirty hit that sent me flying into the boards also sidelined me with a concussion. It didn't end there. More bad luck plagued our team. Nolan went into a scoring slump, and Benny took a punishing check against the boards that broke his foot. We were knocked out of the playoffs in the first round.

I went to Minneapolis, my hometown, to sulk.

"Next year will be different," my always-positive father tried to reassure me.

He was wrong.

We missed the playoffs entirely the following year, for reasons still unknown.

Then there was the season that just ended this past spring—another disappointment.

LAS VEGAS WOLVES FOLD, KNOCKED OUT ONCE AGAIN IN THE FIRST ROUND

Needing a break from all things desert-life, I said to Nolan and Benny, "Fuck this shit."

That was over three months ago. We were in the middle of cleaning out our lockers for the summer. My linemates looked at me, confused.

And then Nolan finally asked, "Fuck what shit, Oliver? What are you going on about over there?"

"Everything," I replied, gesturing around the empty locker room. "We're done, finished. Let's get the hell out of this place for a while."

I meant Las Vegas the city—and I think Nolan was catching my drift—but Benny misunderstood.

"Dude," Benny began, "we *better* get outta here soon." He checked his watch. "We have a tee time at two."

He meant the golf game we had planned, but I was having none of that.

"Fuck golfing," I snapped. "I'm talking about *really* getting out of here. I think we deserve a much-needed break from this whole damn town."

Nolan looked intrigued. "What'd you have in mind?"

I happily shared with him and Benny what I'd been thinking about for days. "Let's head up to my house in Minnesota. We can spend the summer on the lake." I grinned, bad intentions in mind. "You know I'm a fucking rock star up there. We can party every night. Hell, we can fuck and get fucked up till training camp starts up in September."

Benny was in immediately, but Nolan had to think it over in his thoughtful kind of way.

At last, he said, "Okay, let's do it."

Since that day we've been partying like rock stars. Or, more accurately, like out-of-control hockey players.

We're still on a roll, even though it's August and we have to fly back to Vegas real soon. Until then, however, I've vowed my cool contemporary house by the lake will remain *the* place to party. It's our OPS base for debauchery, after all.

In reality, though, this craziness can't go on. We all know that.

Even wild and crazy Benny had the sense to ask me just last week, "Dude, what should we do?"

"About what?"

I was in the midst of texting a local puck bunny to see if she wanted to meet me for a quickie, so I was a bit distracted.

Benny sighed. "We gotta report to camp in a less than a month. Guess it's time to start thinking about slowing down with the girls, the booze, the—"

I put down my phone and cut him off with a raucous, "Hell no, my friend. We just need to scale it back a little."

"Scale it back in what way?" Nolan, who walked in the room just at that moment, wanted to know.

I shrugged. "Maybe have smaller parties? Maybe drink a little less?"

We all agreed to those things, but we haven't followed through. In the past seven days we've abstained from partying for all of two.

This is so not going to play well with the team. My diet is crap, and I'm nowhere near peak playing shape. Sure, my body looks all lean and cut, meaning you'd never know I wasn't ready to hit the ice rearing to go, but looks can be deceiving. I went out for a run just the other day and came back fucking winded as hell.

That was a first.

Still, I'm confident I can get back into playing shape in no time. It's the inside of my head that's kind of a mess. I just don't fucking care about winning, not anymore. I mean, I do, but I don't. Does that make sense?

Nah, it doesn't to me, either. But I better figure it out, and fast.

Where's my drive to get my shit together? Where's my commitment to winning, my obligation to my players?

I ask myself these things every day now, but I guess the answers are clouded by my drinking copious amounts of alcohol and fucking way too many puck bunnies.

Dad would be so proud—not.

Well, he would be glad I diligently use protection. I haven't gone *that* far off the rails. Still, wrapping my dick up isn't enough to keep management off my ass. My agent already informed me— this morning, in fact—that the Wolves' ownership group has a pretty good idea of what I've been up to, along with my teammates, here in Minneapolis.

I listened half-heartedly when my agent woke me up to say, "Don't blow this off, Brent. Management is *not* happy with you. There's a certain image they expect you to uphold, and you're not doing that."

God forbid I'm not the team's "Golden Boy." I'm "The Next One," remember?

Bullshit, it's all crap.

Coach Townsend called me shortly after I got off the phone with my agent. He had the same warning.

"You don't want the team to take action. You're not going to like what they have in store for you, Brent, if you keep up with this bad behavior."

"Oh, come on," I replied, laughing. "The Wolves can't fire me. And what could be worse than that?"

Coach T chuckled like he knew something.

Hmm…

"I can't worry about that shit today," I said to him. "I'll start cleaning up my act tomorrow."

"Brent…" Coach T sounded doubtful.

"Really, I will," I insisted.

That was a few hours ago. And I plan to make some changes. But maybe not quite yet.

"Before tomorrow gets here," I justify to myself, "we still have the rest of today. And that means there's time for one more party."

I stride into the second-floor living room of my house, a

spacious and angled space overlooking the huge lake on my property. Peering out at the crystal blue water, I announce to Benny and Nolan, "Listen up, boys. We're having one final blowout tonight, a party to end all parties."

There's a murmur from Nolan, but nothing from Benny.

"We're going to do this one right," I go on. "We party tonight. But then, when tomorrow arrives, we're done with messing around. We start training full-on."

Yeah, right, a little voice in my head coughs out.

I look around since no one besides my guilty conscience seems to be chiming in.

It's early afternoon and the sun is bathing the room—my favorite, by the way, with the way it juts out over the lake showcasing the floor-to-ceiling windows on two sides and a massive deck with a mile-long view on the other—in a warm summer glow.

Nolan, who is lounging on an easy chair with a beer in his hand, raises his bottle. "I'm in," he says.

His words aren't the least bit slurred, even though he's been drinking straight through since last night's bash.

"And then, yeah," he continues, agreeing with me, "we'll start getting ready for camp."

Despite his ability to suck down alcohol like a fish, Nolan hasn't veered too far off course. Getting back on track won't be hard for him. He's like Mr. Discipline. And he's not fooling anyone, anyway. I caught him working out in my basement gym a few days ago.

With the way he was pumping iron I suspect he's been training consistently for a few weeks now.

There's still not been a response from Benny, which is unusual. Dude's always up for a party. He's probably the worst of us when it comes to out-of-control antics.

And that's saying a lot.

"Hey, where's Benny?" I ask Nolan as I scan the shadows of the room.

He nods to a sofa that's been pushed way-ass off to a far corner.

"Oh, I should've known." I chuckle as I take in an eyeful.

Benny is sprawled out on a sofa in the shadows, sleeping like a baby. His massive chest is rising and falling in perfect rhythm with the ticking clock on the stone mantel above his head. Some puck bunny he was fucking around with last night is with him, passed out on top of him.

The sheet covering their naked bodies is hiked up just enough to afford a view of the girl's creamy thigh, which is casually slung over my linemate's muscular, hairy-as-hell leg, and positioned under his semi-exposed junk.

Chuckling at Benny's total lack of modesty, I pick up a throw pillow and lob it at his head—the one that clearly controls all his thinking.

And he scores!

As the pillow makes contact—and how could it not with a pole like that marking my target?—the sheet falls off completely.

I get a quick flash of perky tits and tiny ass. And then, shit—a big honking piece of man-meat assaults my eyes.

"Dude," I snort, mock-offended. "You need to cover that shit before you blind us all."

Benny stirs to life. Sitting up, he barks, "What the fuck, Oliver? I was having the best dream ever. That is till you started tossing shit at my balls. "

Nolan lets out a low chuckle. "Only you, Benny, could find a way of using 'tossing' and 'balls' in the same sentence. But really"—he tilts his bottle to Benny's dick—"you need to do what Brent said and cover that shit up."

Throughout this entire brain-draining exchange, the girl wakes up. And damn, she looks young. Letting out a little squeak, not unlike a hamster, she gathers the sheet around her naked self and scurries off to where she seems to think the bathroom is.

I only know this 'cause she's muttering something about having to pee. But the poor girl has no idea where to go. Hamster-girl flies past me, heading down the wrong hallway, the one that leads to my bedroom.

As I rush to retrieve her, I can't help but grumble, "Why in the hell do they always think the damn bathroom's down *my* hall?"

I catch up to and redirect the girl, pointing her in the correct direction. "It's that way, sweetheart," I say in my kindest tone.

No need to be an asshole; the poor thing already looks shell-shocked. Though whether that's due to waking up in a strange house or waking up next to that monstrous thing Benny calls a cock, I have no clue.

"Thanks, Mr. Oliver," she replies.

And then she runs off.

"*Mr.* Oliver?" I shake my head. "What the fuck is up with that? If she thinks I'm old and I'm only twenty-two, then…"

Whoa, wait.

Hurrying back out to the living room and pointing an accusatory finger at Benny, I say, "That chick better be over eighteen, dude. We're in enough trouble already with the team."

Benjamin Perry is twenty-eight, but he likes younger girls. Nothing illegal, so don't get your panties in a bunch. He just happens to favor babes who either look young, or are *just* old enough.

"She's twenty-three," he replies, sounding hurt by my accusation.

"What? Five years past eighteen?" Nolan peers over at me and smirks. "Hey, Oliver, you think Benny is working up to go cougar on us?"

Laughing, I reply, "Seeing as he's on his way to fucking the full spectrum of girls in their twenties, I do indeed think he's secretly working his way up to thirty."

"Small steps," Nolan says.

"Fuck you," Benny interjects. "You're both dickheads."

I put up my hands. "Hey, don't be pissed at me. Take it up with

Nolan. He started with the jokes. I only brought up the chick's age for your own protection. I'm always looking out for you, buddy."

"Yeah, you usually are," he concedes. "And thanks for that." He shoots me an apologetic grin. "You really are a good kid at heart."

I shrug, feeling a little self-conscious at being called a kid. But then I see what Benny is up to, preparing to bust my balls.

Sure enough, the next words out of his mouth are "You do know I mean *kid* in a good kind of way. Like maybe"—he smirks—"a *golden boy* sort of style."

"Ha. Ha," I retort. And since he's enjoying yanking my chain far too much, I shoot him the bird. "Shut the fuck up, man."

Benny may give me a hard time, but his underlying sentiment is genuine. What he said about me being a good guy, like a decent person, is true. Despite all the craziness of late, I want nothing but the best for my friends. And just because I've been fucking up my own life lately doesn't mean Benny's and Nolan's lives have to go down the shitter too.

Really, I probably should've never invited them to Minnesota. I should have come up to the lake house by myself. That would've been the smart thing to do, especially if my intention all along has been to piss away my career.

I don't really want that, though, do I?

No.

I just need some help in getting back on track.

But where would I find something like that?

Ah, fuck it.

"So what do you say, Benny?" I ask, back to focusing on the party. "You in?"

He stretches, covering his dick with the pillow I threw at him. I make a mental note to have all my furniture *and* their decorative accents, especially the pillows, steam cleaned.

Running his hand through his shaggy, dark blond hair, he says, "Am I in for what?"

"Party tonight," Nolan interjects in his usual no-nonsense tone. "One last blowout, and then Brent here says we're stopping with the bad behavior."

I have to laugh. Nolan is only three years older than me, but it's like he's twenty-five going on forty. He's the voice of reason in our crew.

Well, most of the time.

Not today, though. No, today he agrees to go all-out.

With the party plans full steam ahead, we get on our phones, texting and calling everyone we know.

"Tonight we party hard," I declare when we reconvene in the living room.

"Yeah," Nolan says, holding up a freshly opened bottle of beer.

"You mean hell, yeah," Benny corrects, raising the full shot glass in his hand.

"Hell, yeah," I echo, a beer *and* a shot on the table in front of me. "And just so we're clear," I add. "Tomorrow we give up the booze and the women. Tomorrow we start training for real."

The boys agree, and we drink to our plan.

Yeah, tomorrow we'll do all those things…

Read the rest of *Destiny on Ice* now:

Amazon: http://amzn.to/2gL1XC9